A CHI-TOWN MILLIONAIRE STOLE MY HEART 2

KEVINA HOPKINS

Cole Hart
SIGNATURE NOVELS

A Chi-Town Millionaire Stole My Heart 2

Copyright © 2021 by Kevina Hopkins

All rights reserved.

Published in the United States of America.

Published by Cole Hart Signature, LLC.

Mailing List

To stay up to date on new releases, plus get information on contests, sneak peeks, and more,

Go To The Website Below...

www.colehartsignature.com

PREVIOUSLY ON A CHI-TOWN MILLIONAIRE STOLE MY HEART....

Reign walked in her room and sat on the bed. She turned the TV on and flipped through Netflix to find something to watch. She settled on *Gossip Girl*. She ate her food, and once she was done, she grabbed everything that she would need for a shower.

Reign threw her trash away in the kitchen garbage can, then went to the bathroom. She turned the hot water on in the shower, then brushed her teeth until it was the right temperature.

Reign climbed in, taking a quick ten-minute shower. She was tired and couldn't wait to get some sleep. She was glad she didn't have to go to work until noon tomorrow, because she'd only gotten about four hours of sleep because she and Sin kept fucking throughout the night. They had to have gone through at least six rubbers last night. She enjoyed every bit of it, but now her kitty cat was sore.

Reign got out of the shower and dried off, then tied a towel around her body before exiting the bathroom.

Reign went into her bedroom and stood at her dresser, searching for a pair of underwear and a T-shirt to sleep in. She dropped her towel and bent over to put her panties on when she suddenly felt a presence in her room.

"You won't be needing those," a voice said from behind her.

Reign turned around to see who the voice belonged to.

"What the fuck are you doing in here?" Reign asked.

"You know why I'm here." He gave her a sinister smile before hitting her upside her temple with the handle of his gun. He hit her so hard that her vision became blurry, and she fell to her knees as blood dripped from her head. She said a silent prayer, asking God to help her make it out of the situation alive.

❧

Reign looked up at the timer on the back wall and noticed that time was up for the day. She was grateful for that because she felt herself becoming emotional. She had been holding back the tears that were threatening to fall. Every time she thought about that day, all her emotions were heightened, and she still broke down after all these years. That day was the worst day of her life. She was going to have to mentally prepare herself to talk about it out loud in front of hundreds of people.

"Alright, ladies. I'm sorry, but I'm going to have to end things here for the evening. I will pick up where I left off at tomorrow."

Mumbling and grumbling could be heard throughout the room after Reign said those words.

"What? You can't just end it there!" one of the ladies in the audience shouted.

"I appreciate your enthusiasm, but we're on a time schedule, and we still have dinner and other activities on the agenda for today. I promise to go into full detail, and I'll even answer some of the questions you all have," Reign assured them.

Reign walked away from the podium and headed back to her dressing room to freshen up while the MC took over.

As soon as Reign closed the door, the tears she was holding back began to flow like a river. She started breathing hard, and she felt a panic attack coming on. She didn't know how she was going to be able to tell the rest of her story out loud if she felt like her chest was caving in just from thinking about it.

Reign was trying to calm down when there was a knock at the door.

"Who is it?" Reign called out.

"It's me. Can I come in?" Iris asked.

"Yeah," Reign replied as she wiped the tears from her eyes.

Iris walked into the room and closed the door behind her. All it took was one look at her sister, and she ran to her aid.

"It's alright, Reign. Let it all out. I am so proud of you and how far you've come. You deserve the recognition that you're receiving, and you never know who your story can help. I'm here for you, no matter what, and don't you ever forget that."

"I won't. I love you, sis," Reign replied.

"I love you more. Now come on and get cleaned up so we can enjoy the rest of the day."

"Okay. Give me a few minutes. I just need to call and check on the kids."

"Alright, but no more crying," Iris said before walking away.

Reign took a deep breath and grabbed her phone before dialing her husband's number. She wanted to sound like herself so that he wouldn't be worried.

"Hey, my love," he answered on the first ring.

Hearing her husband's voice brought an instant smile to her face. All of her pain and worries disappeared as if they weren't there. She guessed that's what happened when you allowed a real one to steal your heart.

INTRODUCTION
PART TWO

Reign tossed and turned all night. She couldn't sleep worth nothing. She was homesick and missed her family. She was dreading getting up to speak at the event. The last thing she wanted to do was burst out crying in front of everyone.

"Come on, Reign. You have to get up. We have a lot to do before you have to speak," Iris said. Iris drew the curtains back and allowed the sun to beam into the room.

"No. I don't want to do it. I don't feel well. I think someone should take my spot today," Reign groaned.

"That's not an option, Reign, and you know it. How do you think it'll look if the host backed out? You worked too damn hard for this event, so get up and come on."

Reign huffed and puffed before finally climbing out of the bed. She looked in the mirror and didn't recognize herself. Her normal bright-green eyes had a dull shade to them due to lack of sleep.

"I can't go out there like this, Iris. I look like shit." Reign pouted.

"There's nothing that makeup and coffee won't fix. You only have two days left, then you'll be at home with your husband and kids," Iris reminded her.

That made Reign smile slightly, but it wasn't enough to change her mood completely.

Reign took a quick shower, then threw on a pair of black pants and a tank top. She ate a bagel while she waited for her beauty squad to show up. They did her hair and makeup, then she put on a black jumpsuit and a pair of red-bottom heels. She looked at herself in the mirror and smiled this time. She was glad that her glam team had her looking better than she felt.

Reign and Iris left out of the hotel room and headed downstairs to the conference room, where lunch would be served and the next Q&A session would be held.

"What if I get stuck or cry in front of everybody? I'll make a fool of myself," Reign told her sister.

"You should know by now that crying isn't a sign of weakness. In your case, it shows your strength and how far you came. If you get nervous, all you have to do is remind yourself who you are and how far you came."

Reign peeked through the curtains and saw all the people that were there because of her, and all her fears went away. She fixed her crown, pressed her shoulders back, held her head up, and smiled before walking up to the podium. She reminded herself that she was that bitch.

Reign fought to keep her eyes open. The pain that she was feeling in her head was excruciating, and the blood was starting to drip down in her eye. She couldn't believe her biggest fear was about to become a reality. She had been careful over the course of the years. It seemed like once she was finally happy, she got caught slipping. It was like she meant to be broken and miserable. That was the cycle of her life.

"Come on, John. You don't have to do this. It's not too late for you to leave," Reign pleaded with him as she reached out for her towel so that she could cover her body. John's eyes stayed trained on her the entire time. Before she could grab the towel good, he had his gun pointed at her head.

"Bitch, don't even think about it. The fuck I look like leaving before I get what I want? Do you know how long I've waited and plotted to finally get you alone? At first, I was going to give up because I found out you was Nas's girl and he was always coming over, but when your mother told me you two broke up, I knew it was fate. I had gone to the ATM and took five hundred out so that I could give it to your mother. I just knew that was an amount she wouldn't turn down. I mean, you know how much crack she could get with that?"

Reign was about to respond but he cut her off.

"I mean, seriously, I had been taking one for the team sticking my dick in that whore for damn near a year so that I could stay close to you, only for her to tell me she wasn't going to make a deal. That infuriated me because I had no idea when that bitch grew a conscience. She sucked dick and got high for a living. I couldn't show her how enraged I was, so I continued to play my part. I came over on a regular and fed her drugs and dick so that I could learn your routine. The only problem was you haven't been keeping the same routine lately, so when I came today, I thought it was going to be a lost cause again, but luck was on my side. When I heard you come in, I knew I had to start with getting rid of your whore of a mother. Once that was taken care of, I could make my move on you. I was prepared to wait in your mother's room all night if I had to. It seemed like fate when I heard the shower turn on in the bathroom. That was when I creeped into your room and hid in your closet. I figured what better way than to get you to cooperate if you're already naked," John explained with lust in his eyes.

"What did you do to my mother?" Reign asked. At that point, she wasn't thinking about herself anymore. Despite everything her mother put her through over the years, she didn't want any harm to come to her. She had hopes that, in the near future, with the help of her father, her mother would get better, and they could have a stable mother-daughter relationship.

"Don't worry about it. When I'm done with you, you'll be wishing you were with her." John gritted as he pulled down his jogging pants.

Reign threw up in her mouth as she got a whiff of his odor. It was hard for her to explain his scent. It was a mixture of shit and piss. Then the sight of his dick didn't make matters any better. She wasn't an expert in how dicks should look, but she was positive that something was wrong with his. He was about eight inches long, and the base of it was dark brown. The tip was wrinkled and a discolored pink, then there were a bunch of white specs all over it.

John tried to push Reign legs apart with his, but she was holding them together as tight as she could. There was no way in hell she was about to make it easy for him to rape her.

"Please stop," Reign pleaded as tears fell from her eyes. She could no longer hide the fear that she had from the moment she saw him in her room.

"Stop fighting me before I blow your brains out," he threatened as he punched her in the eye. He punched her so hard that she could feel it starting to close. Her body loosened up slightly, and he used that opportunity to make his move.

John penetrated Reign with so much force it felt like he was ripping her open.

"Arrghh, stop! Get off of me please!" she screamed as she tried to close her legs so that he couldn't go any deeper.

"See, bitch, I tried to do this the easy way but you're making it hard," he said. John held the gun against Reign's head with one hand, and he used his free hand to pull something from his pocket. Reign's eyes got big when she saw the needle filled with heroin.

"Okay... I'm sorry... I won't fight you. You don't have to do this. I'll do whatever you want," she cried.

"It's too late now. I gave you your chance, and you blew it." John smirked.

John stuck Reign in the arm with the heroin and released all the drugs into her body. She instantly became calm, and she welcomed the numbness that took over while he had his way with her. All of her hope and strength of getting out alive was gone. She stared into space as he pounded into her relentlessly. Since she was no longer fighting him, he put the gun behind him and held on to her throat with one of his hands and the crook of her leg with the other one. She prayed that he choked her to death so that she wouldn't have to live what he had done to her.

Reign lay there for what felt like hours. She honestly didn't know how long he had been on top of her. One minute, he was stroking her and calling her all type of bitches, then suddenly, the strokes stopped. She figured he must've cum. The next thing she heard was the sound of gunshots. She was expecting to feel the pain shoot through her body, but instead John's body fell on top of hers.

Reign was so numb that she couldn't move, so she didn't bother about trying to push him off of her. She heard someone calling out her name, but the voice sounded so distant she didn't even recognize who it came from.

John's body was removed from Reign's, and that was when she pulled into somebody's arms. She opened her eyes the best as she could and saw it was Nasir. She didn't know if she should thank him for saving her or be pissed because he didn't allow John to finish her off.

Nasir picked Reign up from the floor and laid her on her bed. He covered her up and then pulled out his phone and made some phone calls. Reign stared at the ceiling while he moved around doing whatever he was doing. She felt herself getting lightheaded, so she closed her eyes and welcomed the darkness.

Reign woke up to the sound of machines beeping. She tried to open her eyes but was only able to see out of one of them. The other one had to be covered with something because all she could see was black through it. She tried to sit up, but her entire body was aching. She had an IV in her arm and a bandage wrapped around her head as well.

Reign could hear her father, Mason, and Nasir having a heated conversation across the room.

"What the hell happened to my daughter?" Nathaniel asked.

"I went over to the house to talk to her and found her being raped. I blew his brains out while he was on top of her. She was in a daze and looked like she had been drugged. She didn't say anything when I picked her up. I laid her on the bed and called my people to come help me clean up and get rid of his body. While I was waiting, I saw she was passed out. I washed his blood off of her, but that was it. I didn't want to risk taking away any other evidence, even though he's gone. After that, I went to her mom's room to see if she was home and found her beaten and passed out in the bed. She had a faint pulse, so I brought them both here. The doctors were basically saying that Helen was suffering from an overdose and a concussion from being hit upside the head with something. When I went to her room, she was still out of it."

"Okay, so what did they say about Reign?" Mason asked.

"They didn't say anything yet, because they're going to have to run some tests, but they have to get her permission first. I couldn't exactly tell them that I saw her get raped without having to explain where the nigga was that did it."

"So what did you tell them that happened then?" Nathaniel inquired.

"I told them that I went to go see Reign and found her and Helen passed out."

"Well, she needs to tell them what happened and what the fuck he gave her so that they can run all the appropriate tests. She can even tell them his name if she wants to. She just can't tell them that he's dead," Mason added.

Reign lay in bed and kept her eyes closed while she pretended to be sleep. She wasn't ready to face any of them or talk to them about what happened. She felt dirty and disgusting. She could feel his dried-up semen between her legs.

There was a light knock at the door before it was swung open.

"Hello. Has she woken up to say anything yet? We really need to talk to her so we can figure out what's going on," the nurse said.

"I'll see if I can wake her up," Mason replied.

Reign felt Mason shaking her. She stayed still for about a minute, then slowly opened her eyes. She looked around the room, and tears fell from her eyes.

"Yo, why is she crying? Are you okay?" Nasir asked, concerned.

Reign opened her mouth to speak, but then closed it right back.

"How about you guys leave out and give me a chance to speak with her?" the nurse suggested.

"No, I'm not leaving," Nathaniel told her.

"It's fine. He can stay," Reign finally spoke.

Mason and Nasir left the room, leaving only Reign, Nathaniel, and the nurse.

"Hey, Reign. My name is Nurse Berkley. Your boyfriend told us that he found you in the house passed out naked along with your mother. Can you tell me what happened?" she asked.

Reign looked over at her father before turning her attention back to the nurse. She didn't know why she agreed on him staying in the room. She was starting to have second thoughts about it.

"I went home after leaving from a friend's house. I decided to take a shower before laying down for bed. After I finished my shower, I went back to my bedroom to look for clothes to put on. In the process, I sensed movement behind me. I turned around, and before I could react, I was hit upside my head with a gun. I tried to fight him off of me, but then he shot me up with heroin. He said it was to help me relax so I wouldn't fight him as much. After that, he choked me and started to rape me," Reign explained as the tears fell from her eyes.

"I want to start off by saying I'm sorry you had to go through this. We will do a rape kit on you and have your blood drawn so that we can test for any sexually transmitted diseases. We would also like to start you on a course of antibiotics to be on the safe side so if you did contract anything, we'll be taking care of it right away. We can provide you with an emergency contraceptive if you want us too. We will be keeping you overnight for observation. We want to make sure that the drugs he gave you are out of your system and the swelling on your head is going down properly."

"Okay. Do you know how my mom is?"

"I'm actually not your mother's nurse. I can have someone to check in on her for you though."

"Alright. Thank you."

"Give me a moment to go get the doctor that will perform your exam. Also, it's protocol that a police officer comes to speak with you as well. Is there anything that you need for now?"

Reign shook her head and went back to staring off into space. She felt someone touch her arm gently, and she damn near jumped out of her skin. She looked up and saw that it was her father and calmed down some.

"I'm sorry. I didn't mean to scare you, sweetheart. You were just staring so I wanted to check on you."

Reign was about to respond when Nurse Berkley returned with a doctor.

"Sir, we need you to leave out for a few minutes while we do the examination. Once we're done, you can come back and sit with her," Nurse Berkley assured him.

Nathaniel reluctantly left the room and allowed the nurse and doctor to do their jobs. He felt bad for his daughter because he had no idea how he could help her recover from that situation.

After waiting in the hallway for about thirty minutes, Nathaniel, Nasir, and Mason went back in Reign's room. When they entered, she was looking straight ahead without acknowledging any of them.

"I think you two should go home. She's not going to talk tonight, and they're about to move her to a room. Once she's settled in, I'll send information," Nathaniel said.

"You're going to stay here tonight?" Mason asked.

"Yeah. I'm not comfortable leaving her right now, and I know they're not going to let us all stay. Call your mother and let her know I'll give her a call in a couple hours. Also, see can you get an update on Helen. Find out what floor did the put her on."

"Okay, Pops. I'll text you with the information," Mason replied.

Mason walked over to Reign and kissed her on the forehead before walking out of the room.

"I love you, Reign. I'll be back to check on you in the morning," Nasir said. He kissed her on the cheek, then left the room behind Mason.

Reign and Nathaniel sat in the emergency room for about another hour until they moved her upstairs to a private room. Reign hadn't said a word to anyone since then. Nathaniel was worried, but the nurses tried to assure him it was normal in rape victims.

Reign lay back and closed her eyes. She pretended to be sleep with the hopes that people would leave her alone. She was tired of being asked how she was feeling because the truth was, she didn't know how she felt. She didn't feel anything. Her body was numb. It was like her brain wasn't sending a signal to her body. She felt empty on the inside. The feeling she had was worse than feeling him on top of her.

Reign didn't know how long she laid there with her eyes closed. It wasn't until she heard silence that she decided to open them. She looked around the room and found her father sleeping in a recliner. She had the urge to urinate, so she climbed out of bed and stumbled slightly. She stood there for about a minute, then walked into the bathroom. She handled her business, then went over to the sink to wash her hands and caught a reflection of herself in the mirror. She didn't recognize the person staring back at her. Never had she looked so bad in her life. Her hair was all over her head. There was dried up blood on her face. Her lip was swollen, and there was a big ass knot on her forehead. She could only imagine what the eye they had covered up looked like.

This is all your fault. You should have dressed more appropriate, and he wouldn't have been watching you. You just laid there and let him have his way because that's what you do best. You're worthless and tainted now. No man will ever love you, her reflection taunted her.

"No, it's not my fault. I begged him to stop," Reign replied.

You didn't try hard enough. Now when everyone looks at you, they will only pity you. You saw the way Nathaniel, Mason, and Nasir looked at you. That wasn't a look of love. That was pity. You're a ticking time bomb right now.

"That's not true. Shut up. Shut up." Reign screamed before she started punching the mirror.

"Oh my God, Reign," Nathaniel yelled as he and a nurse rushed into the bathroom. He hurriedly grabbed her hands and put them under the running water. She watched as the blood ran down the drain. She didn't even feel the pain of the cuts in her hands.

Nathaniel and the nurse got Reign cleaned up, then someone came in and strapped her to the bed for her own safety. She didn't try to fight them on it. She just laid there and allowed them to do it, not even caring. She overheard the nurse telling her father that they were going to have to move her to the psych ward for seventy-two hours of observation. She was officially on suicide watch.

$\mathbf{\mathfrak{F}}$ ⠀2⠀ $\mathbf{\widetilde{\mathfrak{F}}}$

R eign sat on the edge of the bed while Nasir placed her clothes and toiletries inside her duffel bag. Her three-day hospital stay turned into a week. The psychiatrist still didn't recommend for her to go home yet, but Nathaniel thought maybe if she was in a more-comfortable setting, she'd start to feel better because being in there wasn't doing her any good. All they were doing was pumping her up with drugs, and she was going with the motion.

Reign stayed in her room all day except for meals and seeing her psychiatrist. Whenever she saw her psychiatrist, she didn't say anything to her. She just stared out into space or kept a blank look on her face. She refused to eat any of the food they offered her. They warned Nathaniel that they weren't going to let her leave until they at least seen her eat something. Originally, she refused, but on the fourth day, she ate bread and drank water for breakfast, lunch, and dinner. They made her do that for three days. After they saw she was keeping it down, they gave Nathaniel permission to sign her out.

"What are you doing here?" Mason asked Nasir.

"I'm here to pick Reign up. She's coming to stay with me," Nasir replied.

"No the fuck she's not. Y'all aren't even together anymore," Mason said.

"That doesn't matter. I love your sister, and she doesn't need to be alone, and she damn sure don't need to be going back to that house."

"She's doesn't have to go back to that house. She can stay with me or my pops so that we can make sure that she's good."

"She'll be good with me. I was there for her when none of y'all asses was, so don't come around now and act like I don't give a fuck about her."

Reign sighed and lay back on the bed while Mason and Nasir continued to argue back and forth. It was something they did for the past two days whenever they were in a room together.

The door to Reign's room opened. She looked up and saw it was her father, then lay back down and closed her eyes.

"Aye, y'all need to cut this bullshit out. Y'all need to get along for the sake of Reign before I ban both of you from being around her. All this bickering and back-and-forth shit is not good for her health. They already didn't want me to take her home. I had to convince them it'd be less stressful and she'd be well taken care of, but with the way y'all acting, y'all proving me wrong."

"I apologize. I don't mean no disrespect, Nate. I'm just trying to be here for Reign and make sure that she's straight. Y'all know where I live at. You can come visit her anytime you want. If it comes a time that she wants to leave, I won't hold her hostage," Nasir reassured them.

"Fine. She can go home with you, but I swear to God my sister better be safe at your crib. I will be doing pop-ups to check on her too. If I feel like she's not getting any better, we're coming to pack her up and take her with us," Mason warned him.

"Man, I feel you, but you don't have to worry about any of that shit. I'm going to look out for her, and Blake is there too. Deja already volunteered to come stay with her if we're not there."

"Okay, cool," Mason replied.

Once Nathaniel finished signing all the paperwork, everyone left the hospital. Nasir tried to make small talk during the car ride to his house, but after the first five minutes of her not responding, he got the hint and left her alone.

Reign wasn't being completely mute with them still. She was giving one- and two-word answers but only if she felt it was a relevant question. If anyone asked how she was doing, she completely tuned them out altogether.

Nasir parked in his driveway and grabbed Reign's bag from the trunk. He walked around to open her door, but she was already getting out. He hit the lock button on his car, then used his keys to open the front door. They walked into his house, and she walked straight to his bedroom. She saw tote buckets stacked up around the room, but she thought nothing of it and lay across the bed.

"The tote buckets are full of your stuff. I didn't grab everything, but I got the main things you needed and the stuff that looked valuable," Nasir said.

"Thanks," Reign replied dryly. In the back of her mind, she was trying to figure out when he had time to pack up her things and bring them to his house when she'd just agreed a couple hours ago that she was going to stay with him. If she was in the mood to talk, she would have asked him. It would be one of the questions she saved in her mind for a later date.

The truth was, she wouldn't have minded staying with Mason or her father. The only reason she came with Nasir was because he asked her. Being that he saved her life, she felt like she at least owed him that much. Besides, anywhere was better than having to go back to her house.

"I'm about to order some food. Is it anything specific that you want?" Nasir asked.

"No. I'm not hungry," Reign replied.

Nasir flopped on the bed and pulled out his phone so that he could find somewhere to order food from while Reign looked through her totes and found her clothes so she could shower.

Reign walked out of the room and headed to the bathroom. She turned the water on in the shower as high as it would go. She stripped out of her clothes and brushed her teeth. She examined her face, and it was mostly cleared up now. She could tell once she got the stitches taken out of her forehead, it was leave a scar. Luckily for her, it wasn't as bad as she thought, and it was close to her hairline.

Reign climbed in the shower and stood directly under the water. She allowed the hot water to burn her skin, but she didn't flinch not one time. She still felt dirty because this was the first real shower she'd taken since everything happened. The water at the hospital wasn't hot enough for her. The water massaged her body, and she felt herself relax. She sat in the tub and pulled her knees up to her chest. She wanted to get out of her funk because she had a week left before she started school, and she wanted to start on time.

Reign was in the shower for about twenty minutes when she felt somebody shaking her. She jumped until she saw that it was Nasir.

"Why are you shaking me?" Reign asked.

"I was knocking and calling your name, but you didn't answer. I wanted to make sure you were okay."

"You don't have to worry, I'm not going to try and kill myself," she grumbled.

"I didn't say you were." Nasir sighed and turned the hot water down, then got her shower gel and spoof to help her wash up. Once he was done, she climbed out and wrapped a towel around her waist and hair.

They made it to his room just as the doorbell went off. Nasir had no idea who would be at his door, because though he'd ordered food, it shouldn't have been there so soon. Reign started to get dressed while Nasir went to answer the door.

"What are you doing here?" Nasir asked Faith.

"I was at home bored and saw that you weren't on the block, so I thought maybe me and Junior could come spend time with you like we did the other day. You can chill while I cook, then we can watch a movie, and once he's sleep, we can have dessert," Faith flirted.

"Our son can stay, but you have to go. You can't just be popping up over here whenever you want to. Reign lives here with me now," Nasir admitted.

"Since when? I thought you and that bitch broke up," Faith yelled.

Nasir looked behind him to make sure Reign wasn't around, then he stepped outside and closed the door.

"Don't bring your ass over here getting loud. I never told you that we were broken up. I told you our relationship was complicated at the moment."

"So how the fuck y'all transition from shit being complicated to moving her in with you?" Faith asked, getting louder.

"Shut the fuck up. It's none of your business. Just know that she lives here, and shit will be back to how it used to be until I tell you otherwise."

"Fuck you and that bitch. I guess I'll go somewhere else and find some dick. Keep your son. I'll let you know when I'm ready for you to drop him back off," Faith snapped.

Nasir watched as Faith stormed to the car and snatched their son and his bag from it.

"Stop pulling on him like that before I fuck your dumb ass up," Nasir threatened.

Nasir took his son from Faith and walked inside the house. He took him to his room, where Reign was curled up lying down. As soon as he put his son down, he crawled over to Reign and tapped her on the face.

"Hey, lil' man," Reign said with a slight smile. She pulled him close to her and hugged him as a tear fell from her eye. Nas hated that Reign was in so much pain and there was nothing he could do about it. He had already killed the nigga responsible for hurting her, but that didn't lessen her pain. He was now wishing he would have tortured his ass first.

When Nasir saw John on top of Reign, he blacked out. Without thinking or asking questions, he aimed to kill. There was no way he would be able to sleep at night knowing he allowed that nigga to live. He couldn't believe that someone would violate his girl like that. Even if they weren't on good terms, that was still his baby, and she was off limits. Fucking with her felt like he was being tested. He'd never allow someone to be able to brag about hurting her. Part of him wanted to leave Helen where she was, but he knew Reign would never forgive him for that. Even though John was dead, he still wanted Reign to talk to him about what happened, but she flat-out refused. All he could do was give her time though because he feared if he pushed her, she'd go spiraling.

Nasir sat with his son and Reign until the food came. Even though Reign said she didn't want anything, he ordered her some cream of broccoli soup with a couple breadsticks. He wasn't about to allow her to starve herself to death.

"Here, eat all of it too. It's the only thing you have." Nasir handed her the food, and she rolled her eyes before she started dipping the bread in the soup and taking small bites. He watched and made sure that she ate it all. Once she was finished, he handed her a bottle of water. She drank all of it, then laid down in bed and closed her eyes.

Nasir finished his food, then stripped his son down to his T-shirt. He turned on ESPN but put the TV on low so he wouldn't disturb Reign. He wasn't sure if she was trying to go to sleep or shutting down again.

Two hours into watching ESPN, Junior had fallen asleep, so Nasir got up and went to put him to bed. When he made it back to his room, he stripped down to his boxers and climbed into bed next to Reign. She started to stir in her sleep.

"Stop... You don't have to do this. Please... I'm sorry. You're hurting me," Reign cried.

Nasir could tell she was having a nightmare, and he was positive she was reliving what happened that night.

"Baby, wake up. You're just dreaming," Nasir said as he shook her.

"I said stop," she screamed before she swung her arm, hitting him in the face.

"Damn, Reign. What the fuck," Nasir yelled.

"I'm sorry. Are you okay?" Reign asked.

"Yeah. Just go back to sleep," Nasir grumbled.

Nasir grabbed his phone and walked out of the room. He walked into the bathroom to check his face, then walked into the living room. He grabbed a bottle of Henny from the bar and rolled a blunt. He was going to have to be high and drunk to maintain patience in order to deal with Reign.

Nasir sat on the couch and chilled for about an hour until his cell phone dinged.

Sheila: I'm outside. Come open the door.

Nas: Outside where? I'm not at the trap.

Sheila: I know. You told me you'd make time for me today to give me some dick, so I came to you.

Nas: You're outside my fucking house?

Sheila: Yeah. So are you going to come open the door or not?

This was one of the main reasons why Nasir needed to move. He planned on working on his relationship with Reign, but bitches all of a sudden decided they want to do pop-ups and shit.

Sheila: Hellooooo... Are you still there?

Nas: Come around to the back.

Nasir turned the volume up some on the TV, then got up from the couch. He went into his bedroom and saw Reign curled up on the edge of the bed sleep. He went inside his drawer and grabbed a clean pair of boxers and a rubber.

Nasir left his room and walked into the bathroom. He put the boxers on the stand and turned the cold water on in the shower and hooked his phone up to the Bluetooth speaker before easing out of the bathroom. If Reign woke up, she'd think he was in the bathroom, but he doubted she'd miss he was gone anyway.

Nasir walked through the laundry room to his garage and opened it.

"Where did you park your car?" Nasir asked.

"It's on the street," Sheila replied.

Nasir pulled Sheila into the garage and closed it shut.

"Don't come to my house again without talking to me first. Next time, I'll leave your ass out there," he warned her.

"Okay I'm sorry. In my defense, I did try calling but you didn't answer."

"I was busy with my son," Nasir responded.

"Oh, my bad. Are we going to go inside, or are we going to just stand out here and talk in your garage?"

Nasir turned on the garage light, then grabbed Sheila by the arm and led her inside of the laundry room. He locked the door and turned the light off before pulling down his boxers.

"You talk too much. Come put this dick in your mouth," Nasir told her.

"You want me to suck your dick in the laundry room?" Sheila asked.

"Yeah. Is that a problem?" he inquired with a raised eyebrow.

Sheila squatted in front of Nasir and placed his semi-erect dick into her mouth. She bobbed her head and licked him like a lollipop. He grabbed a handful of her hair as he fucked her face until he was cumming down her throat.

Nasir lifted Sheila's dress and bent the top half of her body over his washing machine. He stared at her glistening pussy before putting the condom on. He ripped her thong off, and without warning, he slipped inside of her, causing her to cry out. He had to keep his hand over her mouth to keep her quiet before she woke Reign and his son up.

Nasir was deep in her guts for about twenty minutes before he came inside of the condom.

"Damn. That was so worth the drive." Sheila smiled.

"Good, because you have to go," Nasir said as he pulled up his boxer.

"What? Are you serious? I just got here," she whined.

"I don't care. My son is here right now, and I need to be spending time with him. I'll get back up with you in a few days when I have some free time on the block, then we can be together longer."

"Okay. I'm going to hold you to that too," Sheila said.

Nasir walked Sheila back out through the garage, then rushed to the bathroom. He flushed the condom, then switched the water from cold to hot. He took a quick five-minute shower and dried off. He walked back into the living room and turned the TV off before walking back to his room and climbing in bed with Reign. He had busted a nut, so now he was ready to get some sleep until his son woke up.

3

Nathaniel walked into his bedroom and grabbed his wallet from the dresser and stuck it in his back pocket.

"Are you working from home today?" Amelia asked as she looked up at her husband.

Nathaniel had on a pair of blue jeans with a black button-up shirt and a pair of black leather Giovanni Milan shoes instead of his normal suit and tie for work.

"No. I'm not working today. I'm about to head to the city. I'm not sure what time I'll be back yet."

"You're going to see Reign this early?" Amelia asked.

"No. I'm going to the hospital to check on Helen, then go by the store to buy some things for Reign, then sit with her for a couple hours."

"I get why you're going to see Reign, but why are you visiting Helen? This is the third time you're going to see her. She brought all this on herself and Reign."

"The other days I went, they had her sedated. They told me if I came early, they'd allow me to see her and wait to sedate her. I'm going to fill her in on what's going on with Reign and suggest she goes to rehab."

"What makes you think she's going to listen to you?"

"I don't know if she's going to listen or not, but I have to try. Helen is Reign's mother, and she loves her. With everything that's happened, Reign needs something that will help trigger a positive emotion in her. Right now, she's just a shell in her body."

"I mean, that's understandable, but try not to push her."

"I'm not going to push her, but at the same time, she still plans on starting school next week, so it's my job to help her find some normality. If that means drive to the city every day to convince Helen to get help, that's what I will do for my daughter. I owe them both that much."

Amelia sighed and sat on the edge of the bed.

"I just think that you're wasting your time, and steady going to see Helen is going to give her the wrong idea."

"What idea am I giving her? It's not like I'm visiting her in her house alone. She's laid up in a hospital with IVs and shit. I'm trying to help her, not fuck her," Nathaniel yelled.

"Well, it's not like it would be the first time you fucked her behind my back," Amelia snapped.

"I apologized for what I did all those years ago. I can't take it back, and I'm not about to have this conversation with you. I have to go. I'll see you when I get home," Nathaniel said before walking out of the room.

Nathaniel didn't understand why Amelia was acting the way she was. Helen wasn't a threat to her. He hadn't thought about Helen in that way in years. He honestly just wanted to do everything he could to get her help. His main focus was and still is Reign's mental health, and a part of him knew Reign wasn't going to be okay until she knew her mother was.

Nathaniel grabbed his keys from the key hook and headed out to his car. He had about an hour drive, so he called his assistant to discuss some things during the drive.

Nathaniel pulled up to Rush Hospital and handed the valet driver his car keys before going inside. He stopped at the main desk and got a visiting pass, then headed to the gift shop. He bought two dozen flowers, a couple balloons, and a teddy bear. He got on the elevator and headed up to the fifth floor. He walked to Helen's room and took a deep breath before going inside.

Helen was sitting up, looking at the TV when he walked over to where she was and sat down. She turned her head and looked at him. She opened her mouth to speak, then closed it. She squinted her eyes to make sure she wasn't seeing things.

"Nate, is that you?" she finally spoke, shortening his name like she used to.

"Yeah, it's me, Hells," he replied, calling her by the nickname he used to call her. She was Hells when she was calm, and when she was going off on him, he'd call her Hell Raiser because she didn't know when to stop.

"What the hell are you doing here? I haven't talked to your ass in damn near thirteen years," Helen snapped.

"I'm here because we need to talk about some important things."

"What could we possibly have to talk about? You told me how you really felt about me and my daughter when you told us to fuck off in that two-paragraph ass letter."

"I'm sorry, Helen. You have every right to be upset, but I'm here because of Reign."

"I don't need your apology now. I probably would've appreciated that shit back then, but it's too late now. As for being here for Reign, you're a little too late for that as well. She's eighteen years old now, and she's learned to live without you in her life."

Nathaniel sighed and sat in the seat next to Helen's bed.

"I'm going to tell you like I told Reign. It isn't too late for me to apologize. I take full responsibility for my fuckups. I was selfish back then, and I allowed myself to miss out on Reign's life. I'm trying here though. Reign needs both of us. We failed our child, Hells."

"When did you talk to Reign? And don't tell me that I've failed my child when I was the one that stuck around. I raised her the best way I could on my own. I don't need you coming here and judging me."

"I'm not trying to judge you, Helen. I'm just going by what I've observed over the past few months. I met Reign a few months ago, and she agreed to give me a chance to be a part of her life."

"So you basically bought my daughter? Reign isn't just a forgiving person."

"I didn't buy her. I actually have a bank account open for her that she hasn't accepted yet. When my kids and wife found out about Reign, Mason reached out to her, and she got to know him and my Iris before deciding to let me in. I wasn't sure if she'd told you or not," Nathaniel explained.

"No, she didn't tell me, because she knows better to bring your name up in my house. Just because she's talking to you doesn't mean that I will, and it damn sure doesn't give you the right to give me parenting advice. Reign and I have an understanding. She stays out of my hair, and I stay out of hers. It's worked for us all this time, and I'm a firm believer in if it's not broke, don't fix it."

Nathaniel couldn't believe what he was hearing. The Helen he knew was never so careless. She prided herself in perfection, and she always put other people feelings before her own. Now that he thought about it, that was probably why it was so easy for him to leave her because he thought she would just bounce back like she always did.

"That's the thing, Helen. This shit is broken. There's no reason why our barely eighteen-year-old child should know how to survive without us or stay out of our hair. I'm not just blaming you; this is both of our fuckup. The night you ended up in here, Reign was attacked as well. Physically, she's doing better, but mentally, she isn't there. She needs both of us to get through this, and the only way we can do it is if you get help, Helen. Our daughter is hurting right now, and as much as you think she doesn't need you, she does. She might not tell you, but she told me that she wished you two could have a better bond. We have to face the fact that our daughter is older. We might have fucked up with her, but one day, she's going to have kids, and I don't know about you, but I want to be in my grandkid's life. We both know Reign won't allow you anywhere near them while you are smoking and snorting that shit," Nathaniel ranted.

Nathaniel studied Helen's body language and facial expression. It was hard for him to read what was going through her head. She remained quiet for a few minutes before tears started to fall from her eyes.

"How is Reign doing? I know you might think I'm the worst mother in the world, but I do love my daughter. When you first got locked up, I was good. I used Reign for strength, and I had your parents there to help me while I worked. I figured I could go a few years without you in our lives and once you got out, everything would be good. Even if me and you weren't together, you were a great father to Reign, and I was always able to count on you." Helen sighed as she wiped her tears away.

"Helen, I'm—" Nathaniel started, but Helen cut him off.

"No, just listen. I gave you your turn to speak. Now it's mine. When you sent me that letter, it broke me. It had me questioning everything we shared together, not to mention you not only broke up with me, but you broke up with our child. It was like I never knew you because the Nathaniel I knew loved his daughter. I thought maybe it was a phase or you were going through in jail and when you got out, you'd see how wrong you were for what you did, but that time never came. I was also selfish back then because I felt like if you didn't want our child your family was only helping because they pitied us," Helen said, looking up at him.

"A couple years went by, and I could no longer afford the mortgage, bills, or expenses of the house, so I had no choice but to move into subsidized housing when Reign was about seven. It wasn't the lifestyle I was used to, but I made it work. I couldn't afford daycare, so I worked around Reign's school schedule so that I could keep food on the table and have clean clothes for us. I wasn't happy, but I was content. About two years later, I was lonely and ready to date. That was when I met Leon. Had I known what I know now, I would have never given him my number that day in the park. Our relationship was great for the first couple of years, but then he had a car accident, and something snapped in him. He became mean as hell all of a sudden. Reign doesn't know this, but he used to beat my ass almost every night. He'd hit me in places that weren't visible. The beatings stopped, and the next phase of our relationships introduced drugs. He started giving me the pills he was taking. He told me it would keep me calm, and as long as I was calm, he wouldn't have a reason to hit me."

"Damn, Hells. I am so sorry," Nathaniel said solemnly. He stood from his seat and sat on the bed next to her and held her hand.

"You have nothing to be sorry about. It was being weak and naïve that put me in that situation," Helen replied.

"I'm curious though. If you started off popping pills, how did you end up turning to crack and heroin?" Nathaniel asked.

Helen let out a breath before answering his question. She had never talked to anyone about this before, so the conversation was taking a toll on her because it was making her realize how bad she had fucked up.

"Leon ran out of pills, and the doctor wouldn't prescribe him any more. He came home one day with some crack. I was confused at why he had it, but he told me he found a new alternative to get high, and it took away all of his pain. He convinced me that it would help with my depression, so I thought *what the hell*. At first, we did it in moderation, and it became our secret. Leon had work during the day, so he only did it at night. Meanwhile, I didn't have a job, so I became 'friends' with other people that did drugs and hid it from Leon," Helen said, putting up air quotes around the word *friends*.

"Fast-forward some time, I started to lose weight, and Leon

suggested that maybe I should slow down so he didn't share his drugs with me every night anymore, so while he was asleep, I used to sneak out to find some. My friends got tired of getting me high for free, so that was when I started turning a few tricks for drugs. I got away with hiding it for a few months, but then word got back to Leon, and the nigga dumped me. He told me being with a crack whore would mess up his reputation. The last part of my dignity left with him the day he walked out of my house. I felt like I was a lost cause. I had lost you, and I wasn't even fucking good enough for an undercover crackhead. I became reckless and started letting the niggas come to my house, mainly when Reign was gone or in bed. One day, I was so depressed and didn't have any crack, but one of my friends that did heroin was chilling with me. He convinced me to try it, and I almost died. That was the day that Reign found out I was on drugs. I felt like it was a blessing in disguise because that meant I didn't have to lie or hide it from her anymore. I never did heroin again after trying it that day," Helen explained.

"Helen, the day Nasir found you passed out it was from a heroin overdose," Nathaniel told her.

"I know. John came over like he usually does. We had sex, and he tossed me a few dollars and a baggie of crack. I thought he was going to leave like he normally does, but he said he wanted to kick it and go another round. I didn't think anything of it, so I smoked my shit while he watched TV. While watching TV, he got to asking me where Reign was and when would she be home. I told him I wasn't sure, because she had been gone a couple days. He dropped the subject, and we went back to watching TV. Then he randomly pulled a wad of money from his pocket and handed it to me, talking about it was for when Reign comes home. All he needed me to do was stay out of his way and give him a few hours with her. I flat-out told him hell no. That wasn't an option. I had sobered up real fast and told him he had to go. He didn't like that, so he picked up his gun and pistol-whipped me. I tried to fight him back, and that only further angered him, so he grabbed a needed that I didn't even know he had from his bag and stuck me with it. He kept shooting me up until I stopped moving, then he started fucking my restless body until I passed out. I guess it was my karma for all the shit I had done and put Reign through. I really thought I was going to die that day, and I welcomed it," she stated with no emotion.

Nathaniel couldn't hold back anymore. He pulled Helen into his arms and released the tears he was holding. His heart broke for her. No matter what she did, she didn't deserve that shit to happen to her. She was a victim just like Reign was. He had never been in love with Helen, but a part of him always had love for her, and that wouldn't change.

"Look, Helen, you didn't deserve that to happen to you the same way Reign didn't. I need you to get up out of here, and I'll check you into rehab. I'll pay for everything for you. Once you're better, I'll get you your own apartment. I'll pay the rent up for you for six months. I'll also get you a job at one of my companies so you'll be able to afford all of your rent and bills. This will be your chance to start over."

"What about Reign though? Where is she? What did he do to her? Where is he now?" Helen asked question after question.

"Reign was attacked that night when you passed out. He raped her and hit her in the head with his gun. She didn't give full details of what actually happened that night. She stayed in the hospital for about a week because she had to be observed in the psych ward. She's staying with Nasir right now, but I doubt it lasts because from what Mason told me, they weren't together anymore before the incident happened. She starts school next week at Loyola, so I'll start looking for her a place close to her school when she's ready. I'll cover her rent and bills for the apartment the same way I do for Iris. As far as John goes, you don't have to worry about him anymore. That's already been taking care of. All you have to do now is worry about getting better for yourself so that you can be in our daughter's life."

"What about your wife? I know she can't be okay with this," Helen said.

"I just said all you have to worry about is getting better. I'll deal with Amelia when the time comes," he replied seriously.

Nathaniel knew he was going have to listen to Amelia's mouth, but he refused to make the same mistake twice. This time around, he needed to be there for Helen and Reign. It wouldn't take away everything that he'd done over the years, but it was a start.

4

Reign was tired of laying in bed, so she got up and went over to Nasir's weed stash. She grabbed some weed and rolled up a blunt before going to the living room to grab the bottle of Patrón. She walked back to the bedroom and turned on the radio. She sat up in bed with her back against the head and threw a pity party for herself. It was the only thing she'd been doing for the last couple of days since she'd been at Nasir house. He'd go out outside early in the morning, and she had no idea when he came home, because she barely saw him or felt him get in bed. He barely texted or called to check on her, and she didn't bother about reaching out to him. She was just going through the motions.

Reign had picked up on smoking and drinking more. At first, she used to take a couple puffs of a blunt and be good. Now she was facing two or three of them a day and drinking liquor as if the answers to her problems were at the bottom of the bottle. It was the only thing that seemed to numb her pain because it put her to sleep. As long as she was sleeping, she didn't have to think about how pitiful her life had become.

Blake did try to keep her company sometimes, but she wasn't much company to him, because she was never in the mood to talk. She hated being around him because he had a look of sorrow in his eyes. She hated how people felt sorry for her. That was something that she never wanted.

Reign got faded for about an hour, then felt herself starting to nod off, but the sound of the doorbell interrupted her. She wasn't expecting anyone, so she tried to ignore it until the sound of her phone went off. She picked it up and sighed when she saw the *come open the door* text from Nathaniel.

Reign put the phone back on the stand and climbed out of bed. She put a pair of leggings over her boy shorts, then walked out of the room and opened the door.

"Hey. Can I come in, or do we have to stand on the porch?" Nathaniel asked.

"Hey. I'm sorry. Come in," Reign replied. She stepped to the side and locked the door before sitting on the couch.

Nathaniel set the bags he was carrying down on the table along with some flowers and a bear before sitting down next to her.

"When was the last time you've eaten a real meal, Reign? You look like you've lost weight," Nathaniel pointed out.

Reign had to think for a minute. She was trying to remember the last real meal she'd eaten. She only ate soup the first day she came home a couple days ago, and then she at a sandwich yesterday and today.

Nathaniel sighed as he looked over Reign. The fact that she had to think about when she had her last meal said a lot. He needed to get his daughter out of Nasir's house and fast. He was starting to hate that he allowed her to make the decision her own, but he didn't want her to resent him. He wanted her to be able to make decisions on her own, but it was time that he gave her a little tough love. It could either backfire or him, or it could be just what Reign needed to get it together.

"I ate a ham sandwich today. I haven't really had an appetite," she said.

"You haven't had an appetite, but you can drink and smoke?

Your eyes are bloodshot, and I smell the alcohol seeping through your pores. At the rate you're going, you're going to end up back in the hospital with an IV in your arm. I understand shit is hard right now, but you have to take better care of your health, Reign. What happened to all the goals you set for yourself?"

"What if I don't care about any of it anymore? What if I want to just curl up and die?" she cried.

"Reign, you are stronger than this. I know you've been through a lot at your age that you shouldn't have, and I played a part in that. I take full responsibility for that, and that's why I can't sit here and listen to you talk like this. If you fall into depression, you are allowing him to win all over again. Despite what happened, you're still capable of achieving all your goals. I know I can't tell you to stop drinking and smoking, but you need to slow down. If you can't do what you need to do, I will drag your ass out of this house and take you back to that psych ward. I brought you home so you could get better. Not pick up a new fucking habit that could kill you faster. I just had a long ass conversation with your mother. She's getting discharged in a couple days. I'm going to pick her up and take her to rehab. I'm not sure how long she will have to be there, but she agreed to stay until she feels better. During that time, I have to find her a place to live. You said you wanted her to get help, so I need you to help me see her through this. I just need you to meet me half-way. So tell me what's it going to be, Reign. Are you going to try and get better at home, or do you want to go back to the hospi-tal?" Nathaniel asked. He looked into her eyes so that she could see that he was serious.

"I don't want to go back to the hospital. I will try to get better. I'm just so confused right now. I can't tell if I'm coming or going. I know I'm not an angel, but I try my best to do good by people. I just don't understand why I was dealt this hand. Why would he do this to me, Dad," Reign asked as she broke down and cried.

Nathaniel cried right along with Reign as he pulled her into his arms. He was so happy that she had finally called him "Dad". He just wished that it was under better circumstances, but he had to take what he could get.

"Don't you dare sit here and blame yourself. The man that attacked you is the only person to blame. You don't have to get through this alone. Allow your brother, sister, and me to help you. Please don't allow this situation to push you away from us."

"I won't. I know that I need you all's help. I just didn't want to be a burden, which was one of the main reasons I ended up here with Nas. If it's not too late, I'd like to take you up on that offer and help me find my own place. I'll pick up more hours at work so that I can help pay the bills."

"It's not too late for me to help you find an apartment. You just have to tell me when you're ready to look, and me or Mason will help you. I don't want you picking up more hours at work. I want you to be able to focus on class. I paid for Mason's room and board while he was in college. I'm paying for Iris's room and board too, so the same will go for you. The money that I would have had to pay for you to stay on campus will go toward your apartment. Those funds don't have anything to do with the money already in your account. You're free to do whatever it is you want with that money."

"Okay. I'll accept it, but it's for emergency purposes right now, and once I finish school, I'll use it to start my business."

"Alright. Whatever works for you, I got you. Now go take a shower and do something to your head while I cook you something to eat."

Reign stood from the couch and showed Nathaniel to the kitchen. He took the bags of groceries he brought with him and got to work while she got herself together. She came in the kitchen about an hour later to him making her plate. He had cooked a chicken and shrimp fettucine with garlic bread. Everything smelled and looked great. She hoped it tasted as good as it looked because the aroma of the food had her mouth salivating.

She didn't realize how hungry she was until she saw and smelled the food.

Nathaniel put their plates on the island, and they sat down together to have dinner. This was their first time spending this much time alone, and surprisingly, it wasn't awkward for either of them.

"Oh my God. This tastes so good," Reign groaned as she ate her food.

"I'm glad you like it. I made enough for you to have some left over."

"Thank you. I really appreciate everything that you're doing for me. I know it might not seem like it, but I am grateful, and in the short time that you've been back in my life, you have helped me tremendously, and I'm not just talking about financially. You're helping me learn how to open my heart and mind up for the idea of forgiveness."

"You're welcome, princess, I'm just glad that you're giving me the opportunity to be here for you when you need me the most."

"I know I start school next week, but I was wondering if it would be okay to probably go to your house this weekend?" she asked nervously.

"Reign, you can come over anytime you want. Hell, I'll help you pack and move your stuff in today if you want." Nathaniel laughed but he was dead serious.

"Nah, I don't want to move in with anyone else. I think it's best if I have some time to myself to try and focus on getting back to a better version of me. I really just want to work and focus on school right now."

"Okay. Well, text me what kind of apartment, condo, or house you want, and I'll get in contact with my realtor tomorrow for you."

Reign and Nathaniel sat around and talked for about another hour until he headed home. Reign cleaned the kitchen and went into the room and turned the radio back on. She grabbed her journal and sat back in bed. For the first time since she'd been staying with Nasir, she welcomed the silence. It gave her a chance to reevaluate her life and write out her new goals. She was happy that her mother was going to get herself clean, and she was going to do everything that she could to make sure it stayed that way. She thought about if she should just tell her father to look for one place and she share with her mother so she could help be her support system. It was something she'd give some thought to. She didn't want her mother to get lonely and fall off the wagon.

Reign had fallen asleep in the middle of her writing, but was woken up when she felt a dip in the bed. She looked over at the clock and was surprised Nasir was home by eleven.

"Reign, are you woke," he asked.

"I am now," she mumbled.

"I'm sorry for being gone so much the last couple of days. Some shit went down at the trap house that I had to take care of, and you know I got that work from your brother, so I had to get everything situated. If you're up to it, I want to take you out to breakfast in the morning," Nasir said.

"Okay. That's fine," Reign replied.

Nasir and Reign remained silent until Nasir pulled her close to him and started to kiss the back of her neck. It all made sense why he came home early. She wasn't in the mood for sex, but she'd do it if it meant he would be off her back. In order for her to make the moves that she wanted, she needed him to think everything was good between so he wouldn't have to keep a close eye on her. She needed to make her next move her best one.

Nasir slid his hand in between her legs and played with her clit until she was wet. He took that as a sign that he could keep going. He pulled her panties down, then took his boxers off and hovered over her.

"I missed having sex with you, Reign. We haven't fucked in months," Nasir said.

"I know because you don't know how to act right. Can you put a condom on first?" she asked.

"Why do I have to put on a condom? I been pulling out all this time," he stated.

"Circumstances are different now. We're in an open relationship, I don't know where your dick been, and I start school next week. I'm not taking the chances of getting pregnant before I graduate."

"Really, Reign? You still talking about this open relationship, but you're sleeping in my bed every night," he yelled.

"Nigga, that's right, I'm sleeping in your bed every fucking night alone, so either put the condom on or get the fuck off of me," she snapped.

"Man, this some bullshit. This why I be staying out now," he grumbled before grabbing a condom from the nightstand and rolling it on.

Reign didn't give a fuck about Nasir's attitude. It was time for him to see that it was her way or no way. He was no longer the one to dictate how shit went in their relationship.

Nasir shoved his dick in her with no warning, and her mind immediately went back to John raping her. Nas was fucking her like he was aiming just to get his nut off, and she didn't like it at all. She couldn't even get into what he was doing. She closed her eyes and tried to think of anything besides him being on top of her. It seemed like he wasn't going to stop anytime soon, so she started fake moaning to see if it would speed up the process.

Nasir flipped her over on her stomach and slammed back inside of her. She welcomed the change of position because now she didn't have to squeeze her eyes shut. She could just stare at the headboard in front of her. After fifteen minutes, she was tired of faking her orgasm.

"Are you ready to cum yet?" she groaned. He didn't say anything, so she started to throw her ass back on him. She wasn't enjoying the sex, but she knew how to make him to cum. He only lasted two more minutes before she felt him pull out of her. She was about to get up when she felt him hold on to her waist and released his seeds all over her ass and back. She sat there and let him get that one off because it was no telling when she was ever going to have sex with him again.

"Are you happy now? I finally came," he said.

"Yep," she replied, popping the p.

Reign climbed out of bed and went straight to the bathroom to take a shower. She scrubbed her body and wanted to cry because Nasir made her feel the same way John did that day, and if sex was going to be like that for her from now on, she was going to be celibate. She was hoping the reason she didn't enjoy the sex was because she wasn't feeling Nasir like that anymore. She didn't want her rape to have ruined sex for her for good because that meant when she was ready to settle down, she wouldn't be able to properly satisfy her husband.

Reign walked back into the room and saw Nasir getting dressed. She smelled his shower gel, so that meant he showered in the other bathroom.

"You're about to go?" Reign asked.

"Yeah. I have something to take care of. Don't wait up," he replied.

"So you only came home so that you could fuck me?"

"No, I came home so that I could spend some time with you, but you have a fucking attitude, and I don't feel like dealing with the shit. I'd rather be in the streets taking care of business. It's not like you care if I'm here or not," Nasir growled.

"You're right. I don't give a fuck. You didn't even have to come here to fuck me. I was good without it. You could have kept giving it to whatever bitch you been giving it to," Reign said.

"Maybe I will." Nasir smirked before grabbing his wallet and walking toward the door.

"Fuck you, Nasir," Reign yelled. She picked up a book from the nightstand and threw it. He tried to duck, but he wasn't quick enough, and it hit him in the head.

"Let me get the hell out of here before I fuck your ass up. I'll see you later," he spat.

Nasir walked out of the room and slammed the bedroom door. All Reign could do was chuckle to keep from crying. She couldn't believe how drastically her life had changed. She was tired of crying over spilled milk though, and she refused to shed tears over Nasir. It was no time for her to do what was best for her. Fuck what anybody else thought about it.

5

THREE AND A HALF WEEKS LATER

It was Saturday evening, and Reign was sitting in bed studying. Even though she'd only been in class for a little over two weeks, she wanted to stay ahead of her studies. She was back to working and starting to feel like herself again. She wasn't one hundred percent yet, but with a little more time, she'd be there. She slowed down with drinking and smoking like her dad asked her to. She made sure to eat at least two meals a day and work out. She gained three pounds back. She wanted to gain the other seven pounds she had lost back.

Nasir walked into the bedroom and started slamming drawers and making unnecessary noise. She didn't want to have to deal with him, but if she wanted to get any work done, it was best to acknowledge him or he won't stop.

"What's up, Nasir? Is everything okay?" Reign asked.

"No, it's not. It's my motherfucking birthday, you won't give me no puss, and you not going out with me tonight. Something is fucking wrong with this picture. What am I supposed to say when the guys ask where you at?"

Reign dropped her pen and looked up at Nas.

"I know you not doing all this over me not giving you no pussy. Why can't you get it from whatever bitches you been fucking the last few weeks?"

"Here you go with this shit. I told you I been out working, so I don't know where you are getting me fucking other bitches from, and that still doesn't explain why you don't want to celebrate my birthday with me tonight."

Reign shook her head and chuckled lightly as Nasir fed her his usual bullshit.

"Nasir, you already know I'm far from dumb. I just don't trip over the dumb shit because we both know I will go toe to toe with your ass. The fuck I look like letting a nigga slide between my thighs that can't keep they dick in their pants or bring they ass home at night? The last time I brought up you going to fuck the bitch you been giving it to, you smirked at me and said 'maybe you would'. You haven't attempted to touch me since then, so I know that you were serious. As far as going out to celebrate your birthday, I'm not feeling it. I don't want to be in a crowd, and I don't want to be around your fake ass friends. I refuse to embarrass myself or look crazy behind you. They smile in my face and call me 'sis'. Whole time, they are smiling and doing it with whoever else you bringing around when I'm not present. I offered to cook dinner for you or take you out."

"Girl, you the only one thinking that. I don't bring no bitches around them niggas, and I only said maybe I will that day because you pissed me off. I haven't attempted to touch you since then, because your ass been tripping, and the last time we fucked, you didn't even cum for me, so I figured you needed time to get yourself together, so I've been beating my dick," Nasir explained.

It amazed Reign how Nasir could look in her eyes and lie with a straight face. The shit was baffling and downright scary. She couldn't believe she had never seen the signs of his narcistic ways a long time ago. She was blinded by lust because she knew that she didn't love him.

"Okay, well, it won't hurt for you to beat your dick for a couple more days. Make some time in your schedule tomorrow, and I'll take you out. If you can bring your ass home by midnight all next week, I'll let you get some." Reign shrugged.

"Whatever, Reign. You know this some bullshit," Nasir mumbled before storming out the room, but Reign didn't give a fuck. She picked up her ink pen and got back to working like the conversation never happened.

Reign studied for about another hour, then stopped to take a break. She picked up her phone and scrolled to Sincere's number. He had been trying to reach her for the past month, and she had ignored all his calls and text messages. Since she was feeling a little better, she decided to reach back out to him.

The phone rang three times before she heard his sultry voice.

"Hey, stranger," Sin spoke.

"Hey. I know I've been MIA, and I'm sorry for that. I just been going through some shit lately, but I wanted you to know I wasn't dodging you."

"Why didn't you tell me? I could have come back out there to help you get through whatever it is."

"I wish it was that simple."

"It could be if you were willing to let me in."

"I want to trust you and let in, but it's hard. It's just too much going on at once. I don't want to weigh you down with my problems."

"What's going on with you? You don't sound like yourself."

"It's too much, and it's not a conversation to have over the phone."

"Okay. I'm about to book a flight right now. I'll be out there tomorrow to see you so we can talk. You can come out to my house, or I can come to yours. Before you try to protest, I'm not taking no for an answer."

"I'm sorry, I can't..." Regin trailed off.

"Didn't I just say I'm not taking no for an answer?"

Reign sighed as she thought about how to respond to Sin. She didn't know how much she wanted to tell him.

"It's not that. Everything is complicated right now. I can't stay at my house right now, so I'm staying with dude ass, and you can't come here. I'm not trying to drive all the way to your house and then come right back here. I have two classes Monday."

"It sounds like you're making up excuses, so I'm about to make this easy for you. I'm about to book a room at the Hyatt by the airport for the next three days. When you get there, stop at the front desk and give your name. I expect you to be there tomorrow when I land because I'm coming straight there from the airport."

"Sin, you really don't have to do this. I will be fine. Don't you have work Monday?"

"I know I don't have to do it, but I want to. I told your lil' ass I'm ready to show you how you supposed to be treated. I'm willing to do everything that nigga you be laying up with not doing. As far as work goes, I'm bringing my laptop with me. I'll work at the hotel while you at school. Once you finish, you can come back and hang out with me. I'll fly back out early Tuesday morning."

"Alright. Text me the confirmation for the hotel and your flight itinerary," Reign said.

"I gotcha, beautiful. See you tomorrow."

"See you," Reign replied.

Reign couldn't hold back her smile when she hung up the phone. She couldn't believe Sin was willing to fly all the way out there just to check on her well-being. She had the help of her siblings, father, and stepmother, but it hit different when a nigga she hadn't even been knowing that long was willing to be there for her more than the one she'd known for over a year.

"Who the fuck you were just on the phone with that got you smiling like that?" Nasir bellowed, causing her to jump because she didn't notice he was in the doorway. She had no idea how much of her conversation he actually heard.

"Nobody," Reign replied.

"Yeah, a'ight. Don't let nobody get your ungrateful ass fucked up."

"First of all, your ass not stupid. I wish the fuck you would put your hands on me. You better find something safer to play with, and how am I ungrateful?"

"You walk around here like you mad at the world. Meanwhile, some nigga call, and he got you cheesing from ear to ear. If he makes your ass that happy and you don't want to be here, why your disrespectful ass at my house and not his? Then you got the nerve to be sitting here in my bed talking to the muthafucker on the phone that I bought and pay the bill for."

"Nigga, you the last person that should be talking to me about disrespect when you fucked a bitch in this house while I was here. Like I said before, your ass not as slick as you think you are."

Nasir stood quiet with a shocked look on his face. He had no idea that Reign knew anything about Sheila being there. He didn't know how she could have found out, because he made sure they weren't loud. She couldn't have heard them from his room, so he decided to call her bluff.

"Girl, gone somewhere. You just making shit up now. You didn't see me with no bitch in here, so how you gon' say I fucked somebody here?"

"Please stop insulting my intelligence. For once, be a man and own up to your dirt. You fucked the bitch in the laundry room the first night I was here. Your dumb ass thought I was sleep, but I wasn't. I got up to get some water and check on your son. I didn't see you anywhere, but your car was in the driveway, so I knew you were in the house. When I got by the laundry room, I heard the bitch moaning and you telling her she was too loud. After that, I went and laid back down in the bed. You and that ho lucky I wasn't in my right state of mind that night, or I would have gone in there and shot both of y'all asses with your gun for playing with me," Reign snapped.

"Don't try to turn this around on me because your ass got caught. Like I said, if you want to smile and talk to that nigga, find another way to do it. Let me catch you again, and I'm going to disconnect that motherfucking line," Nasir warned her.

Reign stood from the bed because Nasir had her heated. That was the second time he threw some shit in her face, and she wouldn't allow him to get a third time.

"Don't get me wrong, I might have needed your help at first, but I don't need your ass now. These past couple of months, you showed me what kind of nigga you are. As long as a bitch down and out, you in love with them, but the minute they get on they feet, you find a different way to bring them down. I'd rather starve to death and sleep under Wacker Drive with all the other homeless people before I ever ask your ass for help. Your bitch ass really got me all the way fucked up. Fuck you and this phone," Reign yelled.

Reign picked the phone up from the bed and threw it at Nasir, hitting him in the head hard as hell. He rubbed the spot she hit him in. He rushed over to where she was and slapped her ass before she could react.

"I told you to keep your fucking hands to yourself. That slap was just a warning. Next time, I'm going to knock the taste from your mouth," Nasir threatened. He walked over to where her phone was and stepped on it, making sure to crack the screen.

"Nigga, I'll give you that one because I hit you first, but let that be the last time you even attempt to raise a hand at me. And I don't give a fuck about your dumb ass breaking a phone that you paid your money on. I'll just go buy me a new one. The fuck," Reign told him.

"Let me go in the front because you really pissing me the fuck off. I'll liked it better when your ass was mute," he mumbled before walking out of the room.

Reign rolled her eyes and started to get her stuff together. She put her books in her backpack, then grabbed her duffel bag and packed enough clothes for the next three days. Sin wasn't going to be there until tomorrow, but she figured since he booked it already, she might as well put it to use. Once she was finished packing everything she needed, she walked toward the front of the house where Deja and Nasir were sitting down talking.

"Hey, girl. I was just about to come back there and talk to you," Deja said, jumping up from the couch and hugging her.

"Hey. I didn't know you were here," Reign replied.

"I just got here like two minutes ago. I know you not about to go."

"Yeah, I need to catch the phone store before they close since somebody broke my phone, and then I'm going to see my brother."

"Okay. You'll be back in time to go out tonight, right?" Deja asked.

"Nah, I'm not going. I don't want to be around a bunch of fake people, and I done had enough of your brother's shit for one night."

"Girl, I was just in here talking to him about that. Both of y'all asses tripping right now. Y'all keep saying shit just to make each other mad but know neither of you going nowhere," Deja rattled on.

"I'll see you later, Deja. We can probably do lunch one day this week," Reign stated, changing the subject. She wasn't even about to entertain Deja with a response to that because at the end of the day, Nas was her brother, so she was going to forever have his back and take up for him. She was positive that Deja knew about most of the shit Nas was in the streets doing.

"Okay, be safe. Text me when you get your new phone," Deja replied.

"Will do," Reign said as she walked toward the front door.

"Are you coming back tonight?" Nasir asked.

"Nah. You can have fun with whatever bitch you want you want here," Reign told him.

"Gone somewhere with that bullshit. I'm not bringing

nobody back here. It's mighty funny how I catch you on the phone with a nigga and now you supposedly going to your brother house when at first you were sitting in the bed doing homework."

"You don't know who I was on the phone with, and even if I was going to a nigga's house, I didn't think you cared since less than thirty minutes ago you asked why I'm here with you and not at his house. Maybe I'm just listening to your suggestion."

"Bitch—" Nasir started, but Deja cut him off.

"Dude, don't be calling her out her name. You know she don't have another nigga. She just saying this shit to get under your skin," Deja said, trying to reassure him.

Reign chuckled slightly before walking out of the house and to her car. She was going to let Deja think whatever she wanted because she wasn't about to sit there and tell her anything about Sin. Eve was the only person that new about him, and she planned on keeping it the way for now.

6

Eve used the keys Ricky gave her and entered his apartment. She was livid because he was supposed to had picked her up from the nail shop an hour ago, but he wasn't answering his phone. She just knew she was about to walk in on some bullshit. If he was there with another bitch again, she was about to catch a case. She wasn't about to let him off easily this time.

The living room, dining room, and kitchen were empty, so she walked toward his bedroom, and the door was cracked. She peeked through the door and was shocked at what she saw. She would have rather found him with a bitch than seeing him sniffing lines of coke. She pushed the door all the way open, causing him to jump, dropping the piece of paper in his hand.

"Look what the fuck you made me do," Ricky yelled at her.

"Nigga, you shouldn't have been doing the shit any-damn-way. How the fuck are you getting high on your own supply?"

"It's rough out here in these streets. This shit keeps me calm and my dick hard. It ain't made shit change between us all this time, so don't start tripping," he replied.

"Bullshit. I can't believe I fell in love with a crackhead," she snapped.

"Bitch, who the fuck you calling a crackhead? I never smoked crack a day in my life. My girl Whitney said it best: crack is cheap. This shit right here is pure powder. I don't fuck with that cheap shit. so don't put me in the same category as no damn junkie. Just get the fuck out of my face. Your ass blowing my high," Ricky yelled.

"*Bitch*, I'm not trying to hear that shit. You're just an expensive ass junkie," she shot back, putting emphasis on the word *bitch* since he called her one.

Before Eve could continue her rant, Ricky jumped up and popped her ass right in the mouth, causing her lip to bleed.

"Learn when to shut the fuck up. You should know by now not to play with me, Eve. I haven't beat your ass in a while, and I can see you miss it. I bet your pussy wet right now. Get the fuck out of my face and go clean yourself up so you can come back and get what you looking for." Ricky smirked.

"I can't believe you hit me that hard. Talking about come back and get some dick. Your ass better hope I don't chop that motherfucker off," Eve cried before leaving his bedroom and going to the bathroom.

Eve and Ricky had gotten into plenty of fights over the course of their relationship. They had been knowing each other forever since he used to hang out on her block. Over time, they exchanged numbers and started fucking. He had taken her virginity and threatened to kill her or any other nigga if he found out she ever gave it up to anybody else, and she believed him. After that, their relationship became official.

They had been together for almost two years now, so toxicity was the norm for them. Sometimes she was knocking him upside his head, and other times, he was knocking her across hers, but he had never hit her hard enough to cause a bruise or blood before. He would usually just choke or slap her, but he had never hit her in the mouth like that.

It wasn't always like that between them. Their relationship started to shift about six months ago when she first caught him cheating on her. Instead of leaving him, she beat the girl's ass and then slapped him. He allowed her to get away with the first hit, but then she tried again, and he hit her ass back. Afterward, she found herself fucking him in the same bed that she just caught him with the girl in. That alone said a lot about their relationship.

No matter how much Ricky cheated, she stayed faithful and by his side because she knew he loved her and the other bitches didn't mean nothing to him. The thought of letting another man have the part of her that she promised her man would only be for him never even crossed her mind.

Eve was wifey, and no ho was going to take her place. She had invested too much time and emotions in him for someone to come alone once he wasn't down anymore to reap from it. She already knew if she did half the shit Ricky did, he would leave her, and she wasn't trying to take that risk.

Eve knew what she was signing up for when she got with Ricky. He was a lot like her brother Jason, so she was able to recognize the signs. It wasn't like they were married, and he took damn good care of her, so she was content. She wasn't about to sit around and let him do it in her face, but at the same time, she didn't trip about it as long as he kept his hos in check.

Eve grabbed a towel and washed her face. Her lip didn't look too bad. It was just a small cut that makeup could hide. She walked into the kitchen and grabbed an ice pack from the refrigerator, then waked back inside of Ricky's room. He was sitting on the bed jacking his dick.

"Come over here and catch this nut for me," Ricky said.

"Are you serious? You just hit me in the mouth, and now you want me to suck your dick?"

"Yeah. Since you want to keep busting your gums, you might as well bust them on this dick," he told her.

Eve rolled her eyes as she pulled her long weave into a ponytail. She knew it was stupid to suck Ricky off after he hit her in the mouth, but she felt that if she didn't suck his dick, he'd just leave the house and let another bitch do it, and she wasn't having that. She was horny, and she wanted her man all to herself until they had to go to the party.

Eve sucked and fucked Ricky for about forty-five minutes, making him bust twice.

"Do you want me to cook you something to eat?" Eve asked.

"Yeah. It's some wings in the refrigerator thawed out already. Fry them and make some garlic potatoes and corn. I'm about to take a nap. Wake me up when the food done."

"Okay, I got you," Eve replied.

Eve left the bedroom and went to the kitchen. She connected her Bluetooth to the speaker in his kitchen and got to work. She turned on the deep fryer first. While she waited on the grease to get hot, she cleaned and seasoned the chicken. Then she peeled a few potatoes and put them in a pot of water on the stove. Once the grease was hot, she put the wings in and sat down at the table. She scrolled through Facebook while she waited on the food to cook.

About an hour later, Eve was finished cooking everything. She made Ricky's plate and grabbed him a Pepsi from the refrigerator. She walked inside of his room and shook him awake.

"Thank you, baby. I love you," he said as he took the plate of food from her.

"You're welcome. I love you too." Eve smiled.

Eve left the room and went into the kitchen and made her a small plate. She didn't like to have a full stomach when she went out to the club, because she liked to keep room for the alcohol she was going to consume.

Fifteen minutes later, Ricky walked in the kitchen and threw his trash away.

"I have to go to the trap and check on a few things since Nas took the weekend off for his birthday. I shouldn't be no more than a couple of hours. We are leaving about ten, and your ass take forever, so you should start getting ready soon," he told her.

"Okay. I'll be ready by time you get back."

Eve set her alarm for eight thirty. That would give her a chance to get an hour nap in, and the other hour and a half could be used for her to get ready. It felt like as soon as her head hit the pillow, it was time to get ready.

Eve took a quick shower, then applied some makeup and curled her hair. By the time she was pulling her dress over her head, Ricky was walking into the bedroom.

"Where the fuck you think you going with that lil' ass dress on? You look like a ho right now. Take that shit off," Ricky told her.

"No. There's nothing wrong with my dress. This is fit for a club," Eve sassed as she looked at herself in the mirror. She had on a short black bodycon dress that stopped a few inches past her ass. The upper back part was cut out. In the front, the straps were crisscross, only covering her breasts, leaving an opening at her stomach.

"Stop fucking playing with me and take that shit off, Eve. Your ass not leaving nothing to the imagination."

Eve rolled her eyes and walked out of the bedroom. She went to the bathroom and finished the final touches on everything. She didn't give a fuck what Ricky was talking about. She looked damn good, and she wasn't about to change her clothes to please him.

Eve walked back into the bedroom and saw Ricky about to snort some more coke.

"Damn. How much of that do you do a day? How did I miss this shit?" Eve asked, wanting to know the answer.

"Here you go running your fucking mouth again. This why I don't have your ass at my house like this. A nigga can't even get high in peace with your dumb ass here. I see you still didn't take that dress off. Fuck it. Don't worry about it, because you not going anyway."

"Really? You got me fucked up if you think I'm staying in the house after I took the time of doing my hair and makeup."

"Your girl not going anymore, so there's no need for you to go."

"Whatever. Your ass didn't want me to go anyway. That's why you came in here picking a fight. You must get one of your bitches meeting you there," Eve yelled, getting in his face.

Ricky jumped up and grabbed her by throat.

"Shut the fuck up and chill out. You the only one thinking about other bitches. Have your ass here when I get back," he told her through gritted teeth. He let her neck go and walked out of the bedroom.

Eve sat on the edge of the bed and waited until she heard the front door slam, then she grabbed her phone and called Reign.

"Hello," Reign answered on the fourth ring.

"Hey. Why you sound sleep and your man's party about to start?" Eve asked.

"Because I am sleep. I'm not going to that shit. I don't feel like being around any of his people."

"Come on, Reign. I want to go, but Ricky talking about I can't go because you are not and I'll be the only female there," Eve said.

"Girl, I'm not going to no strip club just so you can go. Believe me, you won't be the only girl there because Deja will be there too."

"Fuck this. I'm going. I got to go make sure my man knows how to keep his hands to himself. I'll watch yours too since you are tripping."

"I don't need you doing me any favors. I know who Nasir is. You go have fun though," Reign said, hanging up the phone.

Eve sighed, then put her phone in her purse. She called her cousin to see if she'd go with her to the club, but she had plans already, so she called a taxi and was going to go alone. She already knew it was going to be some shit with Ricky, but she didn't care. She wasn't about to allow him to dictate her moves. She was about to go, and she was going to enjoy herself, whether he liked it or not.

7

Nasir and his crew were celebrating his birthday at the Odyssey Strip Club inside the VIP section. Drinks were going around, and some of the baddest bitches was swinging on the poles and giving out lap dances. His team was having the time of their lives while he was drinking Henny from straight from the bottle. He was trying to drink thoughts of Reign away.

Reign said she was going to her brother's house, but he didn't believe her. He had called Mason, but he didn't answer. He tried calling her, but the phone kept going straight to voicemail. He thought maybe it was because she didn't have a phone yet, and he immediately felt like shit because that meant she was out somewhere without being able to communicate, but that thought left his mind when she replied to Deja's text message. That meant she had him on the block list, so his mood changed from being worried to being pissed.

Yeah, he played hard at the house and acted like he didn't care if Reign fucked with another nigga, but that was far from the truth. He had his speculations, but if he ever found out they were real, he'd be crushed.

Nasir loved Reign. He just had a funny way of showing it. He knew most of the shit he was doing to her was wrong, but at the same time, he felt like as long as he was taking care of home, she should accept it. He made sure her pockets were laced with money and she had the latest shit when it came out. He'd take her on dates when she wanted to go somewhere, and he supplied her with A1 dick and head. He didn't understand why that wasn't enough for her or why it didn't make her happy. He was giving Reign more of him than he had any other female, including Faith. He knew plenty of bitches that would love to take Reign's spot, but he wouldn't give it to him.

Nasir was a young, paid nigga, and he wanted to enjoy the fruits of his labor, which included a few other bitches here and there. He needed Reign to just sit back and be patient with him. He wanted to marry her one day, so that's why he wanted to get all the bullshit out of his system now, and when the time came, he could be a faithful husband and start a family with Reign. Had he known he'd be so close to losing her, he would've bust in her every chance he got so that he could get her pregnant. He didn't really want any more kids at the time, but if he had to have another one, he'd want to have it with Reign. Her mouth was reckless sometimes, but she had a good head on her shoulders.

"What the fuck are you doing here? I thought I told your ass to stay at home?" Nasir heard Ricky yell, pulling him from his thoughts.

Nasir turned to see who he was talking to and saw Eve with a little ass dress on. He perked up a little because he figured if Eve showed up, Reign probably changed her mind.

"I told you I wasn't about to sit in the house after I got dressed. From the looks of it, I got here just in time because you're getting a little too friendly with this bitch. I thought y'all wasn't supposed to touch them," Eve yelled.

"You about to make me fuck you up for embarrassing me in here, and then your hardheaded ass still got that fucking dress on," Ricky bellowed as he grabbed her by the arm and snatched her up out of the section.

Nasir shook his head and sat back in his seat and got back to drinking. He was glad he didn't have to deal with bullshit like that. No matter how mad Reign got, she'd never show her ass in public or let a bitch see her sweat. She'd wait until they were alone and tear into his ass.

About ten minutes later, Nasir was feeling good and tipsy. He was ready to enjoy his night and worry about his problems tomorrow. He pulled one of the girls on his lap and smacked her ass while she twerked on him. She turned around and straddled him, then began to grind.

"I was beginning to think I wasn't going to catch your attention." She smiled.

"Well, as you can tell, you have my full attention now, so what you gon' do with it?" he asked as his dick grew under her.

"Why don't you come with me to a private room so I can show you," she whispered in his ear.

The stripper took his hand and led him out of the section. He saw Eve and Ricky standing by the wall in a heated conversation, so he dropped the girl's hand, hoping that Eve didn't see him holding it.

The girl walked ahead of Nas when she saw the way Eve was looking at her.

"You good, fam?" Ricky asked Nasir.

"Yeah. I just got to make a call to check on some shit at the trap. Hold the section down for me," Nasir replied.

"Nigga, why you standing here lying? Talking about you got to make a call like you didn't just walk out that section with a bitch," Eve jumped in their conversation.

"Yo, get your girl out my business," Nasir told Ricky.

"Bring your ass on. That's why I told your ass to stay at home. Don't be in here minding that man's business."

Ricky grabbed Eve's arm and pulled her toward the VIP section while Nasir walked in the direction where the stripper was. He knew Eve was probably going to tell Reign, but she didn't have any proof, so he wasn't worried about it.

Nasir followed behind the girl until they entered a dark room with a pole and couch. It was where the girls gave private dances, and he was almost scared to sit down because it was no telling how many people fucked on that couch.

The girl pushed him down on the couch and dropped to her knees, unbuckling his belt.

"Was that your girl?" she asked him.

"Nah. If my girl was here, I wouldn't be in here with you. That was one of her friends. Is me having a girl a problem, or are you going to suck this dick?"

The girl answered him by placing his member in her mouth. Nasir placed his hand behind her head to guide her as she bobbed up and down, going further down his shaft.

"Fuck," Nasir hissed as he came in her mouth. She swallowed it, then licked him clean and stood up. His dick was still hard, so she took her thong off and grabbed the condom from her bra and put on him before skidding down his pole backward with ease. She bent over and grabbed her ankles as she bounced up and down. The way she was clenching his dick had him ready to bust already.

"You like how this pussy feel, daddy?" she purred as her juices slid down his dick.

"Hell yeah. You about to make me bust," he grunted.

"You want to nut on my face, baby?" she moaned as she came again.

Nasir had never had a woman ask him that question before. Just hearing those words made him ten times harder. When he didn't reply, the girl smirked and jumped up from his dick and took the condom off. She sucked and then jacked his dick until he was nutting in her face.

"Goddamn, you a freaky bitch. What's your name, ma, and can I see you without that mask over your eyes?" he asked her.

She smiled and took a business card from the stack on the table and handed it to him. He read the name Honey on the card and figured it was her stripper name.

"How about you give me a call the next time you can get away from your girl, and you'll see me without my mask on. You'll have to earn my name though, so for now, you can call me Honey."

"Why do they call you Honey?" Nasir inquired.

"Because I've been told a time or two that's what I taste like. Maybe you can be the judge of that next time." Honey smirked.

Nasir nodded his head but didn't respond. He planned on adding her to his team, but he had no intention on putting his head between his legs. Reign was still the only woman with that privilege. He just had to figure out whose spot he was going to give Honey. It was between Sheila and Faith. He couldn't be spreading his self thin with three other women plus Reign. Maybe he'd just put her on a probationary period first before he decided.

Nasir went to the bathroom and cleaned himself up some and went back to VIP section. Honey entered a few minutes after him and climbed on the pole like they weren't just fucking ten minutes ago.

Eve looked from Honey to Nasir, but she didn't say anything, so he ignored her. He sat back and enjoyed the show. Honey had him ready to leave the club with her that night because his dick was getting hard again, and he knew he wasn't getting no pussy when he got home. He wasn't sure if Reign was home or not, so he didn't want to take the risk of not going home, and he definitely didn't want to show up with somebody.

Nasir stayed at the club until about two, then headed home. When he got there, it was empty, and he was pissed that he didn't shoot his shot with Honey. He didn't know her well enough to call her that late to come to his house, so he sent Sheila a text instead. He knew she would come over since she already texted him and asked if she could see him when he left the club.

Nasir waited for about thirty minutes until Sheila showed up. She was tipsy, so that made his night even better because when they had drunk sex, she allowed him to do anything he wanted to her.

The following morning, Nasir woke up and looked over at the clock and saw that it was a little after nine. Even though he had just gone to bed about five, his body was used to being up in four hours. Nasir looked down at his erection and Sheila sleeping naked on her stomach with her ass tooted you in the air. He needed her to wake up and get out because he didn't know what time Reign was going to be home, so what better way to wake her up then with some dick?

Nasir parted her legs some and slid his dick inside of her. At first, she wasn't moving, but once he was deep inside of her, she arched her back and got on all fours, throwing her ass at him. He fucked her for about a good five minutes, then came.

"Damn, Nas, I didn't even cum yet," Sheila whined.

"My bad. I got you later. The pussy was just too good. I couldn't hold it," he lied. The truth was, he just wanted a quick nut and her out the house.

Sheila perked up hearing him say he was going to spend time with he later. She knew they weren't in a relationship, but he had been spending more time with her, and she was loving every bit of it.

"Do you have plans today? I was thinking we could probably go somewhere since the only time we hang out is at the trap or in the bedroom. Let me treat you for your birthday."

"I got some shit to handle right now, but I'll text and let you know when I'm free."

"Okay, I'm going to go home then, but I'll keep my schedule open," Sheila replied before walking out of the room.

Nasir followed behind her and locked up. He went back in his room and dialed Reign's number, and it was still going straight to voicemail. He didn't want to have to do it, but he dialed Mason's number again.

"What's up?" Mason answered on the third ring.

"What's up, man? Is your sister still at your house? She's not answering my calls," Nas responded.

"Yeah. She's sleep right now. I'm sure once she's ready to talk, she'll answer you. You already know how she is. Just give her some time," Mason told him.

"Okay. Good looking out. I'll have that package for you Tuesday," Nasir said.

"A'ight. Bet. I'll text you a time to meet up. You already know the location."

"Say less," Nasir stated before hanging up the phone.

Nasir was pissed that Reign wasn't answering him, but at the same time, he was glad she was at Mason's crib because that meant she wasn't laid up with some nigga.

Nasir took a quick shower, then got dressed and headed to Faith's house so he could spend some time with his son.

8

R eign woke up to somebody kissing her cheek. She jumped slightly, then smiled when she saw Sincere's face.

"Good morning, beautiful. I ordered us something to eat," Sin said.

"Good morning. What time is it? How long you been here?" Reign asked.

"It's eleven, and I got here about an hour ago. You were sleeping peacefully, so I thought I'd let you sleep a little longer, then I ordered food."

"Thank you," Reign replied.

Reign climbed out of bed and walked over to the bathroom. She took care of her personal hygiene and brushed her hair into a ponytail. She slept in a sports bra and boy shorts, so she just grabbed a T-shirt to put on. She couldn't believe she had slept for almost ten hours.

After she left Nasir's house, she went to the phone store and ported her number to a new phone but got it in her own name. After that, she grabbed some food and went to the hotel. She did some studying, watched TV, then cried herself to sleep around one. Even though she was starting to feel better, she still found herself crying off and on. She mostly did it when she was alone though.

Reign walked out of the bedroom and walked toward the living room area. Sin had booked the king family suite for them, so there was a table to dine at and space where they could set up to do work at the desk. There was also a couch that let out into a sleeper sofa and a wet bar.

Reign sat at the table next to Sin, who was already piling food on a plate. He ordered eggs, breakfast potatoes, bacon, waffles, chicken, and fruit.

"I know it's a lot, but I didn't know what you wanted. I figured if we didn't eat it all now, we could eat the rest if we got hungry again before dinner," Sin said.

"It's fine. You didn't have to do all of this. I would have been fine with some fruit or cereal," she admitted.

"Nah. That's not a good meal. If that's what you are eating in the morning, I need to start having food delivered to you."

"Hey, I'm never one to turn down a free meal." Reign smiled.

Reign and Sin made small talk until they were done eating. She picked up her phone and powered it on. A text from Mason popped up on the screen telling her to call him ASAP. She sighed after reading the message.

"Is everything okay?" Sin asked.

"Yeah. I need to call my brother right quick, then I'm all yours," Reign replied.

Reign dialed Mason's number, and he picked up on the first ring.

"Where the hell are you? You got everybody worried about you. I was about to drive around to see if I could find you. Then you have Nas's ass calling me looking for you. I'm sitting up here lying, talking about you was sleep, but I'm not even knowing where you at or if you were good," Mason rattled on.

Reign felt bad listening to her brother talk. She never meant to make him and her family worry. She should have called them after she got her new phone, but she was so used to looking out for herself that she sometimes forgot to reach out.

"I'm sorry. I didn't mean to make y'all worry. I promise I'm doing okay. I just needed to get away from that house. I'll be ready to look at some of the places Wednesday after I get out of class."

"What did he do? Where are you staying at?" Mason asked.

"Long story short, we got into an argument, and he broke my phone, so I packed a bag and left. I'm staying with a friend until Tuesday morning. I'll be going to class from here."

"Okay. As long as you are good. Next time, just make sure to let us know if you're going to disappear. We know you're grown, but given the circumstances, you have to understand where we're coming from. If you don't want to go back to his house, you can come here."

"Thank you. I understand that. I was in the wrong. I'm going to be more considerate and communicate better."

"What do you want me to tell him if he calls again?"

"At this point, I don't care. You can tell him I'm staying with a friend or that I don't want to talk to him right now. I just need a break from all of it."

"Okay. Well, I won't hold you up from your friend. I'll talk to you later," Mason said.

"Alright, bye," Reign replied before hanging up. She put her phone on silent and placed it on the table. She got up from the table and walked over to the couch where Sin was sitting.

"Are you ready to tell me what's been going on with you? I was on my A game with you, and then you disappeared on me. If I was a weak man, you would have bruised my ego." Sin smirked.

Reign looked at Sincere, trying to decide if she was going to fully open up to him. She hadn't talked to anyone about what happened that night yet, but he was so calm she felt like she could trust him.

"I'm ready to open up and talk to you about myself, but I

don't want you to pity me or look at me differently. I just need you to listen and keep an open mind," Reign told him.

"Okay, baby girl. Take your time," Sin replied. He grabbed her legs and placed them on his lap. He massaged her legs and feet to help her loosen up some.

"I grew up not knowing my father or siblings. He left me and my mom when I was four years old to work on his marriage. He came back into my life a few months ago, but that's another story. Life was hard for us, and eventually, my mother turned to drugs and tricking off. Different men were coming in and out of my house all the time. I had to grow up faster than I should have. I started sleeping with my best friend's brother when I was fifteen because I was curious about sex. In return, he was making sure I was good, so I kept sleeping with him. After about a year, he went away to jail, and that's when I met the guy I'm with now. At first, we started off as friends, then we got into a relationship. He was taking care of me financially, so I overlooked some things, but then I got tired of it. That was about the same time that I met you. I was trying to figure out what I wanted to do, which is why it took me so long to reach out to you. The night I took you to the airport, something happened when I got home," Reign explained as tears started to fall from her eyes.

"You don't have to tell me if you're not ready," Sin told her as he wiped her tears away. He pulled her close to him, and she melted into his arms like she always did.

Reign and Sincere sat quietly for about five minutes while he rocked her back and forth to calm her down.

"I was raped by one of my mother's regular clients. I had a run-in with him a few months ago, and usually, I have my guard up. That day, he caught me slipping because when I got home, it was quiet, so I thought it was empty. I took a shower, thinking about the time that I spent with you, then I went into my bedroom. While I was looking for something to put on, he hit me upside my head with a gun, causing me to fall. I tried fighting him, but he was too strong, and he held a gun at me head the entire time. I guess I was resisting too much for him, so he decided to shoot me up with heroin." Reign paused and turned to look at Sincere. She wanted to look into his eyes to make sure he was pitying her. The look he gave her was of concern, so she continued the story.

"He was choking me while he was raping me, and I actually prayed to God to just let me die so it would end. I don't know how long it went on for, but my ex showed up and stopped him. I wasn't sure if I was happy that he came to my rescue, or if I was pissed that I would have to live with the memories of that night. I ended up passing out and woke up in a hospital bed. They ran tests and everything came back negative, which was the bright side to it all. I had to stay there for about a week though because they admitted me in the psych ward for observation. My dad was scared that I'd try to kill myself because I smashed a mirror in the bathroom and was yelling at myself. Honestly, the thought did cross my mind. All I had to do was pick up one of the pieces of glass and slit my throat, but I couldn't bring myself to do it. All I could think about is if I left this world, my mother would be alone. I was just so angry at the world because it feels like I'm not meant to be happy. It's like my happiness is a curse for bad things to happen to me."

"I am so sorry you had to go through that. You are not cursed, and you do deserve happiness. Sometimes bad shit just happens to good people, and it's out of our control. Where is the guy at now and your mother?"

"The dude is gone. I don't have to worry about him anymore. My mom is in rehab. She should be home in a couple weeks. My dad is getting a place for us to move into. I refuse to step foot back in that house. That's how I ended up at my ex's house. After the incident, I wasn't in my right mind. I wasn't eating or sleeping, so when he offered me to come stay with him, I agreed because I didn't want to be alone. Shit is all bad staying at his house though. It reminds me why me and him could never have a future together."

"Well, I'm glad that your mother is getting the help that she needs. I can keep this room booked up for you until you find a place if you want me to," Sin offered.

"Thank you, but that won't be necessary. I'll be good in a couple weeks, and if things get too bad at his house when I go back, I'll just stay with my dad or brother until I find something."

"Okay. I'm here for you no matter what. Have you thought about going to counseling?"

"Yeah. I just haven't had a chance to set anything up yet. I've been busy with school, working, and not jumping every time someone is five feet within my personal space. Once I find a place and get settled in, then I'll work on finding a therapist."

"Okay. I know now is not a good time, but I wanted to let you know that I'm really feeling you, Reign. I don't pity you or feel sorry for you. If anything, you made me like you more because you showed me how strong you are. All you have to do is say the word, and we can make this happen."

"I like you too, Sincere, but I can't be with you right now. I'm so fucked up in the head that it wouldn't be fair to you. You're too good of a man to be stuck with a broken girl. I need to officially end things with my ex and get out of his house. I need to learn how to love myself and focus on me without the help of a man. I know if I get in a relationship with you right now, you'd do everything in your power to help me out financially, and that's not what I need right now. I'm so used to equating sex and money with feelings that the lines are blurry for me. Don't get me wrong now; I trust and believe that you have my best interest at heart, but I'm not ready right now. I just started school, and I need to focus on that, and you live in Memphis. I can't ask you to quit your job for me. Seeing you one weekend a month would be torture if we were in a relationship because you're the kind of guy that makes a girl want to be up under you whenever she has free time. Any woman in her right mind would love to be in a relationship with you. If I wasn't so fucked up, I could see myself falling in love with you, but the thing is, I don't even know what it means to love someone, because I don't even love myself. I need a friend right now more than a man. I hope you understand and don't spend the next couple of days mad at me."

"It's not the answer I was looking for, but I definitely understand. I could never be mad at you for wanting to get on your shit. I would be less of a man if I didn't want and appreciate that for you. Like I said, I'd be here for you no matter what, whether it's as your man or your friend. I'll help you in whatever way you need. We can still talk on the phone, and when I'm up here, we can hang out if you want to and continue to build our friendship. When the time is right, if it's meant for us to be together, it'll happen. Whether it's in a few months or years."

Hearing Sincere talk like that pulled at her heartstrings because she could tell he was genuinely concerned. If she was a bitch, she'd say fuck everything she said and be with him, but she wanted to make the next relationship she got into right. She wanted to be able to finally fall in love with somebody. She just hoped she didn't just miss her chance at having a good man. She had to be optimistic like Sin and allow the universe to run its course.

Reign and Sincere spent the rest of the day talking and watching movies. They ordered room service for dinner and enjoyed each other's company until about ten thirty, then they decided to call it a night since she had class at nine and he had work. Reign was surprised when Sin didn't try to make a move on her. She didn't know how to feel when he pulled her close to him and went to sleep. She was actually looking forward to having sex with him. She wanted to test the theory and see if she was able to enjoy sex, but obviously, she wasn't going to find out that night.

9

The next day, Reign woke up still engrossed in Sin's muscular arms. She felt his manhood poking her in the ass and unconsciously started gyrating on him. Her love nest was getting wet, so that kind of answered the question about whether she still could. She was thankful for that much, but she still wanted to go all the way.

"Stop moving," Sincere whispered.

"Why?" Reign asked.

"I think you already can feel the answer to the question," he replied.

"What's wrong with me getting your dick hard? You don't want to fuck with me anymore after what I told you yesterday?" Reign inquired, feeling kind of hurt.

Sin lay flat on his back and pulled Reign on top of him so that she was straddling him.

"Reign, if I didn't want you in that way anymore, my shit wouldn't be getting hard just from you being close to me. I wanted to rip your clothes off of you yesterday and make love to you until you couldn't feel your legs anymore," Sin admitted.

"Okay... I don't see what the problem is. Why didn't you? You had me thinking you were mad at me or that I was tainted or something," she stated with a confused look on her face.

"That wasn't my intention, Reign. After the deep conversation we had yesterday, you didn't need my dick confusing you. I didn't want you to feel like you had to have sex with me this trip just because I came out here. I came out here so we could talk. You had me worried about you when I talked to you on the phone, so that's why I dropped everything. It wasn't so that we could sleep together."

"Well, we talked yesterday. Now I want to test a theory and communicate another way," Reign flirted.

"We can't right now, babe. You have to get to school, and I have work to do. I'm not trying to rush or have a quickie, and I don't have any condoms with me."

Reign looked at him to see if he was serious, and his straight face showed her that he was.

"How did you come all the way out here and meet me at a hotel with no protection?"

"Well, I don't just walk around with Magnums and leave them in my suitcase. Like I said, this trip wasn't for sex, or I would have been prepared. It would have been different if we were at my house. My brothers have them scattered around all over the house, and I keep some in my bedroom. Don't worry though. If you still want to do this when you get back from school, I got you. I can go downstairs to the giftshop and buy some. Until then, let me leave you with something to think about," Sincere said.

Sincere flipped Reign onto her back and hovered over her. He kissed her lips, and she gripped the back of his head, trying not to break it. It was taking everything in him not to say fuck it and just give her what she wanted and deal with the consequences later, but he couldn't do that to her. She was in the process of trying to get her life together, and a baby wouldn't make it any better, so he did the only other alternative to hold her over until she made it back, and that was eat her pussy until she squirted all over his face.

Once Sincere was finished, he allowed Reign to go get in the shower first since she was the one that had to actually leave the hotel and he'd probably take longer to shower since he needed to handle his problem. His dick was now rock hard. Reign offered to give him head, but he declined because all that was going to do was make him want to fuck her more. Just thinking about it made him want to kick his own ass for trying to be a gentleman. He had a bad bitch ready to throw him the pussy, and he fumbled because he wasn't prepared. He was definitely going to make it up to her later because as soon as he got a break in work, he was going to buy some protection.

Ten minutes later, Reign walked out of the bathroom with a towel wrapped around her body. Her hair was wet, and drops of water were sliding down her body. At that point, she was torturing him on purpose, showing him what he was missing out on, but he was ready to play the same game with her.

Sincere walked in the bathroom and turned on the shower. As soon as he climbed in, he started beating his meat. He hadn't done that since he was in high school. He was wild the first couple years of college, then he slowed down after that. He wasn't promiscuous anymore, but he did have a couple of women back in Memphis that took care of his needs when they linked up. He was single, so he didn't see the crime in it.

Sin was selective with the women he shared his bed with. He was rich and knew the problems that came along with that. Women threw themselves at him all the time, but he ignored them. He had too much to lose and a reputation to keep for himself. He was the face of not only his business, but his stepfather's as well. He was making money in his sleep, and he didn't have to work as hard. He was only twenty-two, but he was ready to settle down. He wanted a wife and kids to come home to at night after a long day of work. He wanted someone to spoil and share the fruits of his labor with. He wanted all of that with Reign, but she wasn't ready. He couldn't get mad at her for that. He had to remind himself that, even though she was mature, she was still only eighteen.

Sincere wouldn't put his life on hold for Reign, but he had every intention on being there for her if she allowed him. It was like he said; if it was meant to be, no matter the situation, they'd find a way to be together when she's ready, even if it took years.

Sincere shook his head to knock those thoughts off and focused on trying to bust his nut. He thought about the way he and Reign fucked that day, and it only took two more minutes before he was calling out her name as his seeds were going down the drain.

"Did you call me?" Reign asked as she peeked her head through the bathroom door.

"Yeah, but it's okay," Sin replied. He didn't realize he had been that loud.

Sincere hurriedly picked up his shower gel and washed up. By the time he made it in the bedroom, Reign was fully dressed, putting on her jacket.

"I'm about to go. Do you need anything before I leave?" Reign asked.

"No. I'm good, beautiful. I'm about to order breakfast and set up for work. I'll see you when you get back," Sin told her.

Reign kissed Sin on the lips, then exited the room and headed to school. She had three classes, and they all seemed to drag by. She was glad that the day was over, and she could finally go home. She couldn't maintain her focus, and all she could think about was the man waiting in the hotel room for her. That was how she knew she made the right decision of not being with him. She didn't know how to maintain school, work, a relationship, and her mental health right now. She wasn't naïve to believe that Sin would wait around for her. She knew that he would give some woman a good life, and she was willing to accept that because she couldn't string him along like she was doing Nasir.

Even if she couldn't have Sin as her man, she would be grateful to have him as a friend.

Reign left out the school and walked to her car. During her drive, her phone rand. She looked down at it and saw it was Eve.

"Hello," Reign answered.

"Hey, bitch. What you doing?" Eve asked.

"Driving. I just left school. What's up?" Reign countered.

"Girl, nothing. Sitting here at Ricky's house. He told me he and Nasir had some business to handle, so I thought we could hang out since you were going to be alone," Eve replied.

"I needed a break from Nasir, so I'm not going back to his house until tomorrow."

The other end of the line got silent, so Reign took the phone off her ear to see if the call had dropped, but she could still see the phone was still connected.

"I don't know if that's a good idea to wait until tomorrow," Eve finally said.

"Why not?" Reign asked.

"Well, I went to his party yesterday, and when I got there, them niggas were on them bitches like they weren't in relationships. I checked Ricky's ass and stayed there. Nasir dipped off with one of them stripper bitches. I can't say if he fucked her or not, but he did go to a private room with her."

"Why are you telling me this, Eve? This should be even more of a reason for me not to go back to his house."

"I'm telling you this because you're my best friend, Reign. You're giving Nasir too much free time to do him. You have to show him that you care about what he's doing and that you're willing to fight for y'all relationship before he gives somebody else your wifey title."

"Bitch, you sound crazy right now. I know for a fact this nigga is cheating on me, and you're saying I'm supposed to just sit back and play my part. Fuck that. I'm not built like that. Technically, were not even together anymore, so he's free to do him, and so am I," Reign snapped.

Eve couldn't understand how it was so easy for Reign to step out on Nasir and fuck with another nigga after all he had been doing for her. Reign was her girl, so she'd never tell on her, but in a sense, it seemed like Reign was being ungrateful and didn't appreciate Nas. So what if he cheated sometimes? Bad bitches were getting cheated on all the time and still knew their place was beside their man.

"Look, I'm not trying to upset you. All I'm saying is if you can't handle a little cheating, then you don't need to be in a relationship with Nas or any other street nigga. You know the caliber Nas is at now, so it's only going to get worse with the more money he makes. It's not like you love him anyway, so you might as well stop wasting both of y'all's time. As long as you have that 'I don't give a fuck' attitude, that nigga gon' do what he wants to do and stop worrying about your feelings."

"I hear you, Eve, but right now, I don't have to worry about what Nas will or won't do. I should be able to go to sleep at night and not have to worry about if my man coming home or if he's with another bitch. This is not how a relationship is supposed to go. The shit might work for you and Ricky, but it won't fly with me."

"Okay. Well, don't say I didn't warn you. Give me a call when you ready to hang out," Eve said before hanging up, not giving Reign a chance to reply.

Reign knew Eve was in her feelings, but she didn't care. There was no way in hell anybody could convince her to accept the shit Nas was doing. She didn't understand Ricky and Eve's relationship, so that was why she stayed out of it. Everybody was entitled to accept what they wanted in their relationship. She didn't knock or judge anybody for what they tolerated, so she expected the same respect in return.

❧ 10 ❧

Reign walked into the hotel room around 3:30. Sincere was sitting at the desk, typing away on his laptop looking like a Greek god in nothing but a pair of red basketball shorts and black socks. His muscular form and tattoos were on full display. For him to be a businessman, he had the body of a street nigga. She made a mental note to ask him about his tattoos.

"Hey, babe. How was your day?" Sincere asked.

"It was okay. How about yours?"

"It was fine. I've been busy most of the time working. I still have to stay online for about thirty minutes to finish up some things, then I'm all yours. I got something for you on the table in the bedroom," Sin told her.

"Oohhh! What is it?" Reign asked.

"Go in there and find out, girl." He laughed.

Reign kissed Sin on the forehead, then walked into the bedroom. There were a dozen red roses on the table along with an edible arrangement and a box of Magnums. Reign smiled at the gesture. She bit into one of the strawberries, then walked into the bathroom and took a long, hot shower. She loved the way hot water felt when it flowed down her body. It helped relax her muscles and put her mind at ease. When she was done, she wrapped a dry towel around her body. She did her facial routine since she hadn't done it since Saturday, then she took her ponytail holder out and allowed her hair to flow down her back. She dried off, moisturized her body, put on her robe, then left the bathroom.

Reign walked into the bedroom and found Sin sitting on the edge of the bed scrolling through channels on the TV.

"Damn, girl. I thought I was going to have to come check on you," Sin said as he looked up at her.

"Sorry about that. My shower felt so good I lost track of time." Reign smiled.

"It's cool. Did you like your gifts?"

"I did. Thank you. Do you like what you see?" Reign asked as she watched Sin's lustful eyes roam over her body.

The robe Reign had on only went about six inches past her ass, so it showed off her long, thick legs, and the front was partially open at the top, so her breasts were playing peekaboo with him.

"I mean, how can I not when you're standing here in front of me in a robe with nothing on under it? You look sexy as hell, and all I can think about is all the things I want to do to you."

"That's funny because that's all I could think about today while I was in class."

"Well then, how about we stop thinking and show each other," Sin suggested.

"I couldn't agree with you more." Reign dropped her robe and stood in front of him as naked as the day she was born.

"Damn," Sin said out loud as he admired her sexy frame.

Reign smiled at his comment before straddling his lap and kissing him on the lips softly before deepening it. She gyrated her hips slightly, and she could feel his manhood growing under her. Her pussy was dripping wet, and she just knew it was going to be a wet spot on the front of his shorts when she stood up.

Sin broke the kiss and started licking and sucking on her neck, leaving his mark.

"Hmmmm," Reign moaned as his hands trailed up and down her body.

"Are you sure you want to do this? I don't want you to do this just because you feel like you have to since I flew out here. I totally understand if you're not ready," Sin said sincerely.

"You're cute, but you talk too much sometimes. Does it feel like I'm not sure?" Reign asked. She grabbed Sin's hand and slid it down toward her wet love nest. He parted her lips and flicked her clit with his fingers before sliding them further back so they could enter her. He started off with one finger, then added two more. She rocked back and forth on his fingers, and the sounds she was making had his dick hard as Chinese arithmetic.

Sincere played in Reign's love box until she was cumming on his fingers. He removed them and licked one and placed the other in her mouth allowing her to lick her juices off of it. She stood up and helped him out of his shorts and boxers.

Reign licked her lips before kissing his chest covered with tattoos and sucked on his V-line while stroking his dick slowly. She looked into his eyes as she licked from the tip to the shaft before placing him all the way in her mouth.

"Shit," Sin hissed. He threw his head back, and his eyes rolled to the back of his head as she bobbed her head up and down on his dick, twirling her tongue around. She wrapped her hand around the base since she couldn't fit all of him in her mouth and stroked.

Sin grabbed the back of her head, and she hummed on his dick, feeling his dick hit the back of her throat. She used her free hand and played with his balls causing his dick to twitch.

"F-Fuck, Reign. Slow down, ma. I'm about to bust," he warned her as he released his load down her throat.

Reign swallowed every drop, then stuck her tongue out so that he could see. He pulled her up and crashed his lips into hers, not caring that she had just swallowed his kids. He tangled his fingers in her hair and kissed her so hard she had to catch her breath.

Sin flipped Reign over onto her back and stood from the bed. He walked over to the table and grabbed the box of Magnums. He opened them and put one on before walking back over to her. He positioned himself between her legs and sucked on her breast as he took his time sliding inside of her. She closed her eyes tightly as he pushed all the way inside of her. A loud gasp escaped her lips, and then it quickly turned into moans.

"Damn, you feel so fucking good, but I want to see your eyes, or I'm going to stop," Sin whispered as he took his time stroking her slowly because he didn't want to hurt her.

Reign opened her eyes, and he stared into them entire time as he deep stroked her.

"Oh my God, Sin. I'm about to cum," Reign cried out as her body began to tremble. Sin made sure to keep hitting that spot so that she could ride her orgasm.

Sin looked into Reign's beautiful eyes and saw tears. He stopped moving and wiped them away.

"Did I hurt you or something?" Sin asked as he pulled out of her and lay on his back. He was about to take the condom off, but Reign stopped him and climbed on him. She kissed his lips and rode him slowly as tears continued to fall from her eyes.

Sin held on to Reign's waist so she couldn't move anymore.

"What's wrong, babe? I told you we don't have to do this if you're not comfortable. I don't feel right having sex with you while you're crying without knowing what's wrong. I need you to talk to me, Reign," Sin pleaded.

Reign sighed and climbed off of Sin, then turned on her side. She tried her best to hold back her tears, but her emotions were all over the place.

Sin got up from the bed and took the condom off. He tossed it in the trash and then came back. He lay down in the bed facing her so he could see her eyes. He lay there quietly and stroked her hair until she was calm.

"After I got raped, I thought that I would never be able to enjoy sex again. I tested the theory with my ex, if that's what you want to call him, and I hated it. I mean, I got wet, but I wasn't as wet as I normally would be, and I couldn't cum. I literally laid there for about thirty minutes, faking, hoping he would hurry up. The entire time we were doing it, all I could think about was the night I was raped. I didn't know if it was because I don't have feelings for him anymore or if it was just one more thing fucked up with me. That's why I wanted to have sex with you so I could figure out if something was wrong with me," Reign explained.

"Babe, just because you're not feeling sex right now doesn't mean something is wrong with you. But you did just cum twice for me, and I know that for a fact. I can tell if you were faking," Sin said.

"I know. I wasn't crying because I didn't want it. I was crying because I was having a bittersweet moment. Having you inside me felt amazing. My mind didn't go back to that day, so I know it's nothing wrong with me."

"Okay, so why were you crying then?"

"I was crying because in a perfect world, I would be able to make you mine. I have to be one of the dumbest bitches to be willing to give you up when you can please me mentally and physically. I really wish I did have my shit together so this could last forever. When you were on top of me, making me cum, all I could think about was this was probably the last day I get to have you this way," Reign confessed.

"Reign, I will still be coming up here once a month. As long as we're single, I don't see what the problem would be in us linking up. I mean, we both agreed to be friends. Whether we choose to have sex or not is up to us. Let's not overthink things and just go with the flow."

"Okay. I like that idea," Reign said.

"Good. Now lay back and let me finish what you started." Sin smirked.

Reign lay on her back, and Sin kissed all over her body until he made his way to her core. He parted her lips and licked her slit before latching on to her clit. She gripped the back of his head and pushed it further into her pussy. She started to see stars, and she felt her orgasm building up. He slipped a finger inside of her, and she was squirting all over his face within a minute.

Sin grabbed a condom from the nightstand and slid all the way inside her. He bit down on her nipple as he thrust in and out of her slowly. Never had a man been so gentle with her when having sex. He was being caring and thoughtful to her needs.

"You gon' cum with me, beautiful," Sin whispered in her ear.

"Yessss... Go faster, Sin. I'm right there, baby," Reign moaned.

Sin obliged and picked up the pace, making both of them reach their orgasm. Sin's body jerked slightly as his seeds filled the condom. He rolled over and collapsed on the bed.

Reign pulled the condom off of Sin and climbed out of the bed. She threw it in the trash and walked into the bathroom. She freshened up her kitty, then grabbed another towel and wet it with soap and water. She walked back over to the bed and cleaned Sin off.

Reign climbed in bed next to Sin, and he pulled her close to him until they both nodded off in each other's arms. After their nap, Sin ordered room service for them. They ate dinner at the table together in their robes, then spent the rest of the evening chilling and watching a movie until about ten o'clock.

"Let's go take a shower and call it a night. You do have to be up at six," Sin remined her.

"I know. I'm going to miss you though." Reign pouted.

"I'm going to miss you too, but I'll be back up here in two weeks like I already had planned, so we can get together and do something outside of the bedroom," Sin said.

"Oh, but I love what we do in the bedroom," Reign flirted.

"I love it too, but I also love spending time with you outside of it." Sin pulled Reign by the arm and grabbed a condom from the table, then led her to the bathroom so that they could shower.

As soon as the water flowed over their bodies, Sin pushed Reign up against the shower wall and crashed his lips into hers.

"I need you to fuck me, Sin. don't be gentle," she purred.

"Can I feel you without a rubber just for a minute?" Sin asked as he sucked her neck.

"Yes, just don't cum in me," Reign whispered.

Sin lifted Reign's legs up and wrapped them around him as he slammed into her, causing her to whimper and moan with each stroke. The way her pussy was gripping his dick was making him rethink the idea of going in her raw. Her shit was running like a faucet and clung to him like a glove. He tried to focus on making her cum because he knew he wasn't about to last much longer. She had turned his ass into a minute man just that quick. As soon as he felt her warm cum slide down his dick he hurried up and pulled out as he shot his load down the drain. After sliding in her raw once, it was going to be hard going back to using the condoms. That skin-to-skin feeling was on a different level than feeling rubber in between them.

Sincere and Reign cleaned each other up, then got in bed, where they went at it for one more round until they were both drenched in sweat and passed out.

❧ 11 ❧

eign's school day had gone by fast. She got up early that morning, and she and Sincere had a quick sex session before they went their separate ways. She went to school, and he headed to the airport for his flight. She actually paid attention in class and got some work done.

Reign had dance tryouts in an hour, so she was sitting in the student lounge going through the listings her father sent her. She has narrowed the search down to a three-bedroom condo and townhouse. She would have been fine with a two-bedroom apartment, but that wasn't an option Nathaniel showed her. Everything he sent was townhouses and condos.

Reign wanted to make sure she was making the right decision because that would be the place she lived for the next four years, if not longer. She was leaning closer to the townhouse because from the way it was set up, she'd have more space for privacy from her mother. She also needed a spot to practice as well as work out and study in peace. The third bedroom would most likely be a guest room since she planned on getting Mason's daughter Mariah sometimes and if someone visited them.

Reign hoped she wouldn't regret having her mother live with her being that she always said she couldn't wait until she was eighteen so she could get away from her. Reign had a feeling it would be different this time, and usually, her gut was always right. She sent her father a text, letting him know she wanted to see the townhouse that was located on the west side close to the United Center. It was about fifteen minutes from her school and seven minutes from her job. She was excited when her dad texted back and said the agent could show it later on that evening.

Reign was about to scroll her social media when she saw a text come through with the name Bighead and a bunch of emojis. She smiled at the new contact name she saved Sin under that morning. They were talking and agreed using their own name was too impersonal. He had changed her name to Best Friend in his phone with emojis as well.

Bighead: Hey, I'm at home. I actually been here for a couple hours. I meant to text you, but I passed out as soon as I laid across my bed. Somebody wore me out these last couple days.

Me: Well, if you plan something good when you come back, I'm sure you can have a repeat of that over and over again.

Bighead: You already know that's a given. I'll be prepared next time, and I won't be so gentle, so just be ready.

Me: Don't threaten me with a good time. You know that gets my pussy wet. ;)

Bighead: Let me see...

Me: I'm still at school right now. I have dance tryouts, but I'll Face-Time you tonight before bed.

Bighead: You gon' play with it for me?

Me: Only if you play with yours.

Bighead: You know I gotcha.

Me: I have to go now. TTYL.

Bighead: Okay, and good luck on your tryouts. You got this, babe.

Me: Thanks.

Reign placed her phone in her purse and headed to their gym room. She bent over to tie her Air Max shoes when she felt somebody bump her, which caused her to almost lose her balance. Before she could hit the ground, she felt a strong pair of arms grip her waist.

"I am so sorry, lil' mama. I was looking at my phone and wasn't paying attention."

Reign looked up into the face of the fine specimen before her and took a deep breath. He was six feet one and about one hundred ninety pounds of pure muscle with a smooth Hershey's chocolate complexion.

"It's okay. I shouldn't have stopped where people walk in," Reign replied.

"What's your name, beautiful?" he asked, flashing a smile with his perfect white teeth.

"Reign. What's yours?"

"Tavion. I'm the starting point guard. When I get famous, you can tell people you knew me from college. And that I almost knocked you on yo' ass." Tavion laughed.

"I see you got jokes." Reign laughed back.

"I know we just met, but can I get your number?"

Reign debated on whether she should give him her number or not. She wanted to focus on herself and school, but that didn't mean she couldn't have a little fun along the way since she was going to be single.

"Okay, you can get it, but just a heads-up, I'm in a complicated situation that I'm trying to get out of, and I'm trying to focus on myself and school. I'm not looking for anything serious, but we can be friends."

"Okay. I'm fine with us being friends," he replied.

Reign exchanged numbers with Tavion, then headed to the girls' locker room. She went inside and changed into a pair of spandex shorts and a sports bra. She used the lock that she bought and put her belongings up. She could feel a few girls staring at her, but that didn't faze her. She was used to it by now. Not to sound cocky, but if she were them, she'd stare too.

Reign followed behind the girls and entered the gym. It was more girls there than she expected.

"Thank you all for joining us today. As you all know, we have one of the best elite college dance teams. Not only do we dance for the school games, but we participate in national competitions too. We practice two hours a day, five days a week, and some Saturdays if we have a competition coming up. We don't do drama or bullshit on this team. We are looking for serious candidates who enjoy dancing and winning. If any of the things are a problem for you, then you can see your way out the door," Cheryl, the dance coach, explained.

None of the girls moved, so Cheryl continued with her speech.

"We're going to start off with a workout, and then you will learn a routine. There's thirty of you here, but we only have five positions available and two alternates. If I tap your shoulder, that means grab your things and go because you didn't make the cut," Cheryl told them.

The girls all worked out before practicing the routine the captain, Shelly, choreographed. Some of the girls were grumbling because they weren't able to keep up. The routine was on an intermediate level, but Reign worked at a dance studio, so she was already advanced. She was thinking about all the things she could bring to the team to help out with their routines in the future. The captain was a senior, and Reign planned on learning everything she could from her if she made the team so she could have her position next year. She didn't want to be a professional dancer, but she did want to build her portfolio so that it would bring clientele to her studio once it opened.

Midway through practice, a few of the basketball players entered the gym so they could warm up for practice. Reign had no idea they would all share the gym at the same time. She figured there would be a closed audition.

Reign tried to concentrate on her routine and what Shelly was saying, but the guys were starting to distract her. She could hear them commenting on the girls and whistling, only making things worse. Some of the girls were popping their ass a little harder and bending down further than they had to, but all it did was irritate Reign. She closed her eyes to focus for a minute, then got back to work. She wanted to be the best of the best, and in order to do so, she needed to solidify her position by bringing her A game. She couldn't afford any distractions.

When Cheryl blew the whistle, it was time for the girls to show what they learned. The group was broken down into five people at a time. Shelly tapped shoulder after shoulder until she was finally down to her last seven. Reign beamed on the inside when she was one of the last ones standing. She had confidence in herself, but a lot of the girls were really good.

"Congratulations. Welcome to the team, ladies. Reign, Kehlani, Tiffany, Renee, and Bria, you all are the five starters. Lisa and Kelly, you ladies are the alternates. I advise you to enjoy your freedom this week because starting Monday, it's crunch time. I expect you here Monday at three o'clock for practice. You will meet the other ten team members then. Give Shelly your contact details, and she'll email over all of the needed paperwork and contracts," Cheryl announced.

The ladies thanked Cheryl for the opportunity, then gave Shelly their details. Reign grabbed her things and was about to head out when Cheryl called her name.

"Damn," Reign mumbled under her breath as she walked toward Cheryl.

"I know today was only tryouts and you just made the team. I normally don't do this, but I wanted you to know that I watched you at your audition for the dance program here, and I knew then I needed you on my team. I also watched a few of your YouTube videos from high school, and I have to admit I'm impressed. If you keep up the work ethic you have and stay focused, I don't see why you won't be able to have the captain spot next year. Shelly will be graduating and so will the co-captain," Cheryl informed her.

"Thank you. That means a lot to me," Reign admitted as she turned to walk away. She couldn't hide the smile on her face. To say she was surprised was an understatement since, from what she heard, Cheryl had a reputation of being a bitch.

"You must be thinking about me smiling that hard," Tavion said in his deep voice.

"Maybe," Reign flirted.

"So there's going to be a party this Saturday for all the basketball players, cheerleaders, and dance members. It's our way of welcoming all the new recruits since we'll all be around each other a lot, so I hope to see you there," he told her.

"How do you know I made the team?" Reign asked.

"I was watching you tryout. I saw the all the other girls leave. They would have been crazy not to pick you."

"Okay. In that case send me the details, and I'll be there," Reign replied.

"Alright. I have to get back to practice. I'll text you later on with the information." Tavion winked before running off.

Reign smiled, then walked out of school to her car. If she got the house she wanted, everything would start falling back into place like she wanted, then she could start going to therapy. Since it was only five, she had time to grab something to eat and go take a quick shower since she didn't have to meet her father and the realtor until seven.

Reign stopped at KFC and grabbed a two-piece spicy white with mashed potatoes, a biscuit, and a lemonade. After getting her food, she drove to Nasir's house. Since she was coming right back out within the next couple of hours, she parked her car in the driveway.

Reign grabbed her food and bags then went in the house. Blake was sitting on the couch watching a game.

"Hey, sis," Blake spoke.

"Hey. How are you doing?"

"I'm good. You're in for the night?"

"Nah, I have to go meet up with my dad in a couple hours, then I'll be back."

"Alright. I'm in here if you need me," he told her.

"Okie dokie," Reign replied.

Reign sat in the kitchen and ate her food, then went in the bathroom to take a shower. Once she was done, she put on a pair of leggings and a T-shirt with her Jordans. She brushed her hair into a messy bun, then grabbed her keys and purse.

"I'll be back in a couple hours," Reign said before walking out.

Reign drove for fifteen minutes until she pulled up in front of the address. Her dad already texted and said he was inside waiting, so she parked and rang the doorbell. After waiting about a minute, a dark-skinned middle-aged man came and opened the door.

"Hey. You must be Reign. I'm Richard," he introduced himself.

"Nice to meet you, Richard."

"Come on in. Your father is already here."

Reign followed behind him and looked around the house. She loved everything about it. It was a three-level townhome with three bedrooms and three bathrooms and a two-car attached garage. When you walked in, there was a generous foyer on the main level along with the attached garage, large family room with fireplace, and nice-sized private patio. The second level consisted of a huge open living and dining space with a bay window, fireplace, and adjacent bathroom. Completing the second floor was a luxury kitchen with a full line of high-end stainless-steel appliances, granite countertops, and ample cabinet space. There was also a deck off the kitchen for grilling. A full-sized washer and dryer was in there. All three bedrooms, plus two full bathrooms, were located on the third floor. The two-level master bedroom had suite features—an attached master bath with tub, plus separate shower, walk-in closet, and stairs leading up to a huge loft office space with an enclosed storage attic. There was a huge backyard and a massive rooftop deck. She could already see herself chilling up there at night when she needed to think.

"What do you think of it? Do you like it, or should we keep looking?" Nathaniel asked.

"Dad, I love it. You really don't have to get anything this big for just me and my mom."

"I'm sure you two will make good use of the space. It was the least I can do, and I would have been paying about the same price if I got you both separate places, so don't worry about it," Nathaniel replied.

"Well, thank you so much. I already know I'm going to take that master bathroom since I can use upstairs for my office and dance area."

Reign waited around while Nathaniel talked to Richard. After about fifteen minutes of talking and going over paperwork, she was handed the keys to her new home. The only thing left for her to do was order new furniture for the entire house, then she could move in. It all worked out perfectly since her mother should be out of rehab in about a week. Mason and Jordan already packed up Reign's bedroom for her. Everything else in the house was getting trashed. She was going to buy her mother a new wardrobe so that when she started work, she'd look good. The only things of Helen's they were going to take were her mementos like pictures and papers. They were trying to make it so that Reign nor Helen had a reason to step in their old house ever again.

Reign couldn't contain her smile as she headed to Nasir's house. She only had one more week to deal with his shit, then she could be gone. If he pissed her off bad enough, she was going to say fuck the furniture and buy an air mattress until it got there. When Reign got to the house, Nasir's car wasn't there. She was grateful for that. It meant she could talk to Sincere in peace and be in bed by time Nasir got there.

Reign walked in the house and went into the bedroom. She placed her purse on the bed and plugged her phone into the charger. She grabbed her MacBook and headed to the bathroom.

straight to the bathroom. She stripped out of her clothes and called Sin on FaceTime.

"Hey, beautiful," he answered.

"Hey. Guess what." She beamed.

"You made the dance team?"

"Yeah, I did, but this is something even better than that. My dad helped me find a townhome! It's so fucking beautiful. I can't wait until you come out here so that you can see it." Reign smiled.

"Congratulations. I'm so happy for you. Look online and pick out a living and dining room set so that I can buy it for you as a housewarming gift."

"Sin, that is not a housewarming gift. Buying me some dishes or stuff for my bathroom is a gift."

"Girl, as long as it's for your home, it is a housewarming gift. You can't dictate how much I want to spend on it," he told her.

Reign knew she wasn't going to win that argument, so she sighed and was going to let him do him.

"Okay. What is my limit?"

"I'm sure whatever you choose won't break my pockets, so get what you like."

Reign loved Sin's big dick energy because he backed his shit up, and that's why she was willing to bust it open for that nigga anytime he was in town. Just talking to him had her pussy wet.

"You ready to see it?" Reign asked, changing the subject.

"Always. I'm already here naked," Sin said as he pushed his MacBook back on the bed so that she could see his full naked body.

"Damn. I wish you was here with me. I'd deep throat that big motherfucker until I choke. You got me dripping wet right now, baby," Reign purred. She smirked when she saw his dick jump.

Reign set her computer on the stand next to the bathtub and threw her leg across it so that Sin could get a full view of her glistening pussy.

"Fuck. You miss me like that?" he grunted as he stroked himself.

Reign and Sin continued to have phone sex for about ten minutes. She came twice, and he came once. Afterward, they talked about their days before hanging up. Reign closed her computer and took a shower. She did her facial routine and brushed her teeth. She tied her dry towel around herself, then walked to the bedroom.

Reign put on a pajama set, set her alarm, then climbed into bed. It was only a matter of minutes before she passed out.

❧ 12 ❧

Reign was in the middle of a good ass dream. She was cutting the ribbon for the grand opening of her studio when she was woken up by Nasir dragging her off the bed by her ponytail.

"What the hell is wrong with you?" Reign yelled as she jumped up from the floor.

"What the fuck is this shit?" Nasir bellowed as he shoved her phone in her face.

Reign looked over at the clock and saw that it was three in the morning. Her mood turned from irritation to anger.

"Man, give me my fucking phone. I don't touch your shit, so don't touch mine," she snapped.

"Fuck that shit, Reign. I read the messages in here. Who the hell is Bighead?" Nas inquired.

"It doesn't matter at this point," Reign replied nonchalantly.

"It does matter if he's somebody you're fucking. That's who you were with the last couple days?"

"You read the messages, so you already know the answer or you wouldn't be picking a fight in the middle of the night. I guess I should get up and start packing now, huh?" Reign countered as she stood from the floor and sat on the edge of the bed.

"So you got caught up, and now you want to pack and leave."

"Nigga, I didn't get caught up. I told your ass I was gon' do me since you were doing you. It's not my fault if you thought I was joking. The only reason I asked if you want me to pack up and leave is because I don't have time for this shit. I got to get up for class in about four hours. You are sitting here questioning me about my phone when your ass just came strolling in. Let me see what you got in your shit," she told him.

"This not about me. This is about you. How you gon' give another nigga some pussy but can't give me none and you sleeping in my bed damn near every night."

"Man, I told your ass what you had to do if you wanted me to give you some, and you couldn't even do that much. I don't need you to keep reminding me that this is your bed."

"Okay, look, I don't want to argue with you, baby. I fucked up, and so did you. This should make us even. I'll cut them other bitches off, and you can cut that nigga off, then we can act like none of this ever happened."

"What if I'm not ready to cut him off? I mean, you been having your fun for a while now, and I'm just getting started." Reign smirked.

"Stop fucking playing with me and knock that goddamn smirk off your face before I smack the shit out of you," Nasir threatened her.

"Man, you better get out my face. I'm not scared of your ass. I'm about to go back to sleep, or I'm going to start packing. That's my only two options, so what you want me to do?"

"Damn, Reign. It's that easy for you to stop fucking with me? You trying to get back at me or something? I'm sorry, okay? You don't have to keep doing this."

Reign sighed because she really wasn't in the mood to deal with Nasir's bullshit. It was too late or early whichever one you wanted to call it, and she didn't have the energy.

"Nas, don't flatter yourself. I didn't sleep with another man to get back at you. I slept with him because I was horny and felt like it."

"Really? You sitting here acting all nonchalant like you don't care that I found out about you and him. You could at least pretend like you care," Nas yelled as his eyes watered.

Reign tilted her head to the side to see if he was being serious. When she saw he was, she couldn't help but laugh.

"You got some nerve to sit here and cry after you've been out here slinging dick like pussy is going out of style. I know for a fact you done slept with two other women while we were together, and ain't no telling how many I don't know about. You haven't seen me cry one time, so you better suck that shit up," she snapped.

A look of shock and anger washed over Nasir's face as Reign spoke those words to him. There he was laying all his feelings out there for her, and she was telling him to suck the shit up as if it was that simple. He was man enough to admit he fucked up and show her that he wanted her.

"I'm sorry that we all can't be heartless like you, Reign. I told you that I'm sorry. I need you to forgive me. I'm begging you on bended knee right now. I can't lose you. Tell me what I need to do to make this right. I killed a nigga for you, and I'd do it again if I had to. That alone should show you my love is real." Nas laid his head in her lap as the tears fell.

Reign sat there confused because she didn't know what to do. She wasn't used to people crying around her, and Nas was putting on a full show. If this was a movie, he'd win an Oscar for his stellar performance.

"Nas, I have a question, and I don't want you to take it the wrong way," Reign finally said.

"What is it?" he asked, getting up from the floor and looking at her.

She watched as he wiped the tears from his eyes. She could tell they weren't fake, which confused her even more. He had to be sick in the head to have this reaction after finding out she slept with somebody else. This was a different type of psycho. He actually had her a little worried, and she was going to have to tread lightly with her next moves so that he didn't snap.

"Have you ever thought about going to get tested to see if you were bipolar?"

"What? I'm not crazy. Your disloyalty just threw me off guard because I never expected you to do this. It's like my relationship with Faith all over again. I told you she cheated on me, and you went and did the same thing."

"What you not gon' do is sit here and blame me when you the one that started this game, baby. I'm just showing you that I make the rules and can play it better. If you were anything like you were in your relationship with Faith as you are with me, I don't blame her for cheating."

"Okay, Reign. You're right. You can go back to bed now," Nasir told her with an attitude. He stood from the floor and headed for the bedroom door.

"See what I mean? Bipolar. You were just sitting here crying. Now you mad and about to leave the house and go do God knows what with who, and you wonder why I gave a nigga something that was supposed to belong to you. Why would I be loyal to somebody that doesn't have the respect to do the same for me? Every time I say some shit you don't like, you're storming off but expect me to be ready to talk when you are."

"Shut the fuck up, Reign. I'm not leaving the house. I'm about to go downstairs to the basement and chill out because I need to calm down because you got me ready to fuck you up in here," he admitted.

"Well, at least you know to go to work out and not touch me, so you might not be as crazy as I thought," she stated.

"I'll give you that one." Nasir chuckled sarcastically before walking out of the room.

Nasir went downstairs to the basement and lit a blunt. He sat on his couch and threw his head back as more tears fell. He couldn't believe he was actually crying, but he couldn't hide the hurt. He did all of his dirt, but he never thought Reign would pay him back like that, especially while staying under the same roof. He thought he had more time to get his shit together. Finding out Reign was cheating hurt him more than when he found out about Faith. He called it cheating because he wasn't trying to hear that they were in an open relationship since he never agreed to that.

Nasir put his blunt out, then ran on the treadmill for twenty-five minutes and lifted weights for another fifteen. He was still pissed off, but he was calmer. Once he was done, he went upstairs and took a quick shower. He wrapped a towel around his waist, then went into his bedroom, where Reign was sleeping. He put on a pair of boxers and climbed in bed next to her.

Nasir looked up at the ceiling and thought about all the things he had done wrong. His grandmother would be so disappointed in him because she didn't raise him to behave the way he did in the streets. He wasn't ready to get out the game yet, because it was his livelihood, but he could work on fixing things with Reign, and that started with keeping his dick in his pants.

Nasir leaned over and kissed Reign on the forehead, causing her to stir lightly.

"I'm sorry, and I really do love you, Reign. I'm going to do whatever it takes to make things right between us, no matter what," he said out loud before rolling over and going to sleep.

❧ 13 ❧

It was Sunday afternoon, and Reign was sitting on the couch binge-watching *Grey's Anatomy* and indulging in junk food. The week had gone smooth for her, and she was feeling good. She rocked her solo audition and was offered a starting position on the team. She went to the party for the athletes and had a great time. She met all her team members and even mingled with some of the basketball players and cheerleaders. Everyone seemed cool so far. She didn't know if they were always like that or just because it was a party with alcohol involved.

Reign really hit it off with Kehlani. Kehlani was a sophomore, and her drive was on the same level as Reign's. She lived in Detroit but moved to Chicago last year when she got offered a full-ride scholarship for dance to Loyola. She couldn't afford to mess up in school, or she'd lose it all and have to go back home. That was the last place Kehlani wanted to be because she lived a hard life there being raised by her grandmother. Her mother and father were both killed when she was nine. They got caught up in the middle of a gang turf shoot-out. The only family she could live with was her grandmother, and her ass was pure evil.

Tavion was cool too, but she could never see herself getting serious with him. He was your typical jock that looked like he'd tell all his friends you let him hit as soon as he got the chance. He thrived off of the cheerleaders and dancers flocking to him. He loved the attention, and she couldn't be mad at him for that. Around campus, he was HNIC, and females saw dollar signs when they looked at him because he had what it took to make it to the NBA.

Reign had already been with three men that were willing to drop a bag on her without blinking. So the star player of the basketball team with a dream of joining the NBA didn't do it for her. He wasn't even touching any money yet. If she wanted to deal with a cocky playboy, she'd stay in a relationship with Nasir. At least with him, she'd be getting more than just a wet ass.

"Are you feeling better?" Nas asked. He sat on the couch with Reign and handed her a Gatorade.

"Yes, a lot. Thank you," Reign replied.

Reign came in from the party around three in the morning and instantly started throwing up. Nasir was there to hold her hair and help her get cleaned up. He even placed a bucket on her side of the bed and a ginger ale. He got up this morning and made breakfast for her. Ever since he found out she spent that weekend with Sin, it was like a switch got flipped in him. He had come in every night by ten, and he didn't leave the house until after she left for class. It was like he was back to the way he was when she first met him before all of the arguing and disrespect.

Reign and Nasir was halfway into another episode of *Grey's Anatomy* when she felt Nas looking at her.

"Why are you watching me?" she asked.

"I can't help but look. You're beautiful. I don't know what the fuck was wrong with me to mess up with you," Nasir randomly said.

"Don't do this to me, Nasir," Reign replied.

"I'm not doing anything, Reign. I'm just being honest. Let me eat your pussy for you," he requested.

"No, Nas. If I let you taste it, then you're going to want to fuck afterward."

"Yeah, I'll want to, but if you don't, I can't make you. I'd just have to beat my dick afterward." Nas shrugged.

"I can't go there with you right now, Nas. We have a lot to talk about before we cross that line again. Sex isn't going to fix the issues we have in this relationship," Reign told him.

"I know it won't, but I can't help wanting to touch and taste you when I'm around. It's been months since I gave you some head and good dick. The last time we had sex didn't count because I was pissed, and so were you, so you weren't into it."

"I understand that, Nasir. You don't think I be horny too? I miss when we used to be able to have sex, and it just happened. Sex isn't supposed to feel routine, and that's what it feels like when you have to ask me can you taste it or fuck."

"What do you expect me to do if I don't ask, Reign? The way we've been lately, if I touch you without consent, you're liable to pick up something and knock me upside my head."

"That's the point, Nas. It means that we're not supposed to be having sex if you don't even know if it's okay to touch me without permission or not. You're twenty-one years old. You have to know this isn't how a relationship is supposed to go."

Nasir sighed and placed his face in his hands before speaking.

"I know I fucked up, Reign. Everything that went wrong in our relationship is on me. I take full responsibility for it. I swear I'm trying to make things right. I've only been out handling business and coming home. I'm willing to do whatever it takes to fix this, but you have to tell me what I can do, baby," he pleaded.

Reign looked over at Nas and knew he was being honest. She was getting a glimpse of what made her agree to date him in the beginning. Honestly, she was torn between him and Sincere. They were two different people, and she liked them for different reasons, but none of that mattered, because wanted to be single. She didn't want anything serious until she was at least twenty-one. She felt that was a good age to start working on settling down and getting her hoish ways out of her system. It was time for her to have the same conversation with Nas that she did with Sin.

"Okay, you're asking what you can do. Can we have an adult conversation for once without you getting mad or storming out of here? It's time we put everything on the table and lay our cards out," Reign told him.

"Alright, I'm with that," Nas replied.

"First, I want to start off by saying I appreciate that you're willing to change, and I see you trying. I hate it took me entertaining another man for you to be willing to treat me like you're supposed to. I'm going to be honest with you. The guy I spent the weekend with wasn't just some random nigga. I've been talking to him for a few months, and I have feelings for him. I hate to admit it, but I still have feelings for you too, or I wouldn't be sitting in your house. I could have been moved in with my brother or my father."

"What are you saying then, Reign? You want to be with both of us?" Nas asked, confused.

"No. What I'm saying is I can't be with neither of you right now. I have to focus on school and myself. I need to learn how to love myself properly before I can give either of you what you want from me. I'm not in the right headspace to choose a side, so that would result in me fucking both of you over. If I'm being honest, I think the break would be good for both of us so you can figure out what you really want. I believe you enjoy the idea of being with me, but you're not ready to be with me, or it wouldn't be so easy for you to fuck other bitches and then come lay next to me. You need to get everything out of your system because at the rate we're going right now, we'll end up hating each other and ruin the friendship we built in the beginning. I don't hate you, and I don't have any hard feelings toward you. Let's just have a clean breakup."

Nasir sat quiet for about a minute, letting everything Reign said register in her head. There was a lot of truth to what she said about him needing to figure out what he really wanted. He wanted to be the man she deserved, and he hated hurting herm but there was a part of him that wasn't ready for one woman. He enjoyed the thrill of knowing he could randomly pick a woman's name from his phone and she'd sit on his dick on demand.

"You're right. I do need to get my shit together but that doesn't mean I'm going to give up on us. I see the potential in you, and I never want to be the one to break you or stop you from achieving your goals. I do have to admit it's going to be hard having you sleep in my bed without me wanting to touch you."

"I know, but you don't have to worry about that, because I'm moving out tomorrow. My dad found a townhome for me and my mom. The furniture will be delivered in the morning."

"Okay. Can we still stay in touch, and I visit you sometime?" he asked.

"Yeah. I might even let you hit every now and then," Reign said. Even though she was going to be single didn't mean she wanted to be celibate, and she wasn't looking to add a new body to her count unless it was somebody she'd be settling down with, so she figured between Sincere, Jason, and Nas, she'd be good until she figured out what she wanted.

"Well, in that case, you might as well let me taste it before you leave me." Nas leaned over to kiss her, but she stopped him.

"Nah, player. I don't know where your mouth been."

"Shit, it ain't been nowhere. I don't put my lips on no females. Your pussy the only one that's been in my mouth in years," Nasir said honestly.

Reign thought about it and said fuck it. Who was she letting a hungry man starve? She pulled down her shorts and let Nasir feast on her nectar until she came in his mouth twice. After he was done, he got up and went to the bathroom to wash his face and get his nut off.

Reign stood from the couch and went to the other bathroom to freshen up. She came back down and was about to sit on the couch when someone started ringing the doorbell like crazy. She already knew it was about to be some bullshit from the way they were ringing the bell. She looked through the peephole and saw Sheila. She was about to go upside Nasir's head if he'd been fucking around with her since she was Eve's cousin.

Reign opened the door, and there was a look of shock on Sheila's face, so it was obvious she had been fucking with Nasir.

"Reign, what are you doing here?" Sheila asked.

"I live here. What are you doing here?" Reign countered.

"I'm looking for Nasir," Sheila replied boldly.

"He's washing my pussy juice off his face right now," Reign said.

"Wow, so you and him still fucking?" Sheila asked, shocked.

"What's it to you, Sheila? We were supposed to be cool, and you jumped on Nasir's dick the first chance you got just like the rest of the hos on that block."

"Bitch, don't get mad at me because your nigga like fucking me more than he does you."

Reign was about to respond when Nasir came walking her way.

"Who's at the door, bae?" Nasir asked.

Instead of giving him an answer with words, she slapped the shit out of him.

"Bitch, don't be hitting him like that," Sheila yelled before pushing Reign, causing her to stumble back. Reign caught her balance, then slapped her across her face. Sheila reached out and grabbed Reign by her hair.

"Weak bitch." Reign punched Sheila in her stomach twice until she let go, then pushed her down to the floor. She got on top of her and punched her over and over until blood was dripping from Sheila's face.

"Okay, Reign, stop. That's enough," Nasir said, pulling Reign off of Sheila.

"Get your motherfucking hands off of me. So Sheila was the bitch you fucked while I was in the other room?"

"Yeah," Nas admitted as he looked down at the floor.

"Out of all the bitches, how could you fuck her knowing that she's my best friend's cousin? I'm so glad I'm moving out of here. All of them bitches can have your ass. You out here fucking bitches that don't have shit on me, and you know they asses got more miles on they pussy then a 1986 box Chevy."

"Nas, you're just going to stand there and not help me up?" Sheila screeched.

"Nah, because nobody told your ass to come over here unannounced. I told you that we would get together when I called you," Nasir pointed out.

"Well, you haven't called or texted me all week, then when I go on the block, they always talking about you not there."

"Then that should have told you that I wasn't interested anymore. I never old you that we were going to be together. You knew I was with Reign when you kept begging to suck my dick. We were going through some shit, and you helped pass the time," Nasir told her honestly.

"Fuck you, Nasir. You and your bitch gon' get what's coming y'all way," Sheila threatened as she limped her way out of the house.

"Reign—" Nasir started, but Reign cut him off.

"How long y'all been fucking?" Reign asked.

"Off and on for about two months. The first time, I was on some drunk shit, and then the other time was during the month you stopped talking to me. After that, it just happened from time to time. She didn't mean shit to me. She was just always around. I forgot that she was Eve's cousin. I never see them together, so it didn't cross my mind at the time. I was only thinking about myself."

"Go figures," Reign replied. She turned around and walked toward his room. She was about to pack all her things so she wouldn't have to come back to his house again once she moved out.

"You're about to go?" Nasir asked.

"No, I'm making sure everything is together. My brother will be here tomorrow evening to pick up my things. I'm going straight to my house after I get out of class. My dad will be there to let the furniture people in," Reign explained.

"Okay. If you need help, let me know." Nas sighed.

"I will," Reign replied.

Just that quickly, things went back downhill. They went two steps forward only to be knocked ten steps backward.

14

The last couple of days had been hectic for Reign. Between school, work, dance practice, and moving, she was exhausted. She couldn't wait until the weekend so she could get a break and see Sincere. She was ready to go in the house and take a hot shower, then pass out.

Reign used her key and let herself in the house.

"Surprise," Nathaniel yelled.

Reign jumped, then tears fell from her eyes when she saw her mother.

"Mom, you're home," Reign cried as she wrapped her arms around her, hugging her tightly.

"I am so sorry, baby, for everything you hand to go through because of me," Helen whispered in Reign's ear as tears fell from her eyes.

"It's okay, Mommy. You were just sick. We can start over," Reign told her as she continued to hug her.

"I'd like that, baby girl," Helen replied.

Reign stook back from her mother and hugged her father tightly.

"Thank you so much, Dad," Reign said.

"You're welcome, sweetheart. I told you I'd do anything for

you. I'm about to head home and give you and your mother some time to catch up. I'll be back out here in a few days once she's settled to go over some things with her for a job. If y'all need anything else, let me know."

"See you later, Nathaniel. I don't know how I'll ever repay you," Helen added.

"Just bake me one of your famous apple pies, and we're even," he replied.

"Sounds like a deal." Helen smiled.

Nathaniel hugged Helen and Reign, then headed out of the house.

Reign locked up behind her father, then walked back over to her mother. She took a good look at her mother. She couldn't help but smile. Her mother looked absolutely beautiful. During the two months that Helen was away, she gained about twenty pounds, her skin cleared up, and her hair looked healthy. Her curves were more defined. She looked the way she did before she started using drugs if not better.

"You look so beautiful, Mom." Reign smiled.

"Thank you. I feel so good. You don't know how much I appreciate what you and your father did for me. I'm ready to find a job and get life on track. Your father told me that he offered to get us separate apartments, but you suggested we stay together. I promise I won't be a burden, and you won't regret this. I'll help out around the house. I just want you to focus on all your goals. I want to be a mother to you if it's not too late. I know you're eighteen now, so I won't be in your business, and I'll give you space, but if there's anything you need, I'm here for you."

"Thank you. Did you look around the house yet?"

"Nathaniel gave me a tour of down here and the second level. He said he'd let you show me the third one since that's where the bedrooms are and he didn't know which one was mine. I love the living room and dining rooms. The furniture and color schemes are beautiful."

Sincere kept his word and bought Reign's furniture. She had

only sent him a picture of a black dining room set and a black sectional, which cost roughly eighteen hundred dollars from Value City Furniture. He texted her back and asked what her color scheme was. After telling him dark blue, silver, and black, he told her okay.

When she came home from school Monday, she was shocked when she saw the furniture. It wasn't any of the things she sent Sincere. It was more expensive furniture from The Room Place. She loved it, but she didn't want him spending that much money on furniture. He spent almost six thousand dollars on everything. He bought a dining room set plus a full living room set with the coffee table and end tables. He also got her a rug, entertainment center, and a sixty-inch Samsung smart television.

Reign led Helen upstairs and showed her to her bedroom. Helen's favorite color was red, so Reign got her a red and black bedroom set.

"This is your bedroom right here. The guest bedroom is next to yours, and mine is down the hall. I hope you don't mind, but I took the master bedroom because I need the space to dance and for an office."

"I don't care about that. This room is beautiful, Reign. It's bigger than the living room of our old house," Helen said.

"I have one more surprise for you," Reign told Helen. She opened the closet so that she could see her wardrobe, then she opened the dresser drawers as well. Reign spent three thousand dollars on everything Helen would need. She bought her clothes for work, as well as clothes to wear on the regular and night-clothes. She had all new underwear and toiletries. She even bought shoes and a few purses so that Helen wouldn't have anything to worry about.

Tears fell from Helen's eyes as she looked over everything. It had been so long since she had new clothes that she was in complete shock it was all hers. After everything she did, she felt like she didn't deserve what Reign and Nathaniel did for her. She was going to do her best to make them proud of her.

"Thank you so much, Reign. Why don't you go get cleaned up? I'll cook us dinner," Helen suggested.

Reign smiled, then walked down the hall to her bedroom. She took a quick shower, then sat on her bed. She saw Eve called her, so she returned her call.

"Hello," Eve answered.

"Hey. You called?"

"Yeah. I'm trying to find out why would you attack Sheila like that? She had to get stiches over her eye, and you broke her nose. Now I'm beefing with my family because her sister wants to fight you."

"Girl, I'm not worried about Sharon wanting to fight me. I beat Sheila's ass because she hit me first after showing up at Nasir's house and seeing me there. It's not my fault her ass was delusional enough to think he wanted to be with her."

"That may be the case, but you don't even want him, so why should it matter who he fucks with?" Eve asked.

"Are you motherfucking serious right now? It's the principle that she's your cousin and all of us hang in the same damn circle. But in case you didn't hear me, I beat her ass because she put her hands on me first. I beat his ass because he was fucking her. I was supposed to just stand there and let her hit me and get away with it? Fuck that shit. You know that's not how I get down," Reign spat.

"I know, Reign. I'm just saying... I'm in a fucked-up position right now."

"Okay. That's not my problem. You knew Sheila wanted to fuck Nas, so you knew the consequences behind it. You should have told her don't do it, then we wouldn't be having this conversation right now."

"You're right. My bad. I'm just stressed right now, Reign. I have so much shit going on, and I just found out that I'm two months pregnant. My parents and Jason are going to kill me."

"Damn, Eve. I'm sorry to hear that. I have some free time

Friday. Why don't you come over to my place, and we can eat snacks and binge-watch shows until we pass out."

"Alright. I'd like that."

Reign talked to Eve for a few more minutes, then got dressed and headed downstairs. She sat and had dinner with her mother. After dinner, they had a long conversation about everything and decided it was best that they went to family counseling. They would also include Nathaniel in a couple sessions.

⚜

Nasir rolled over and saw Honey was still knocked out. He had taken her out to dinner, then they came back to his place and fucked until they both passed out. He'd been laying low ever since the situation between Sheila and Reign. Sheila had been blowing his line up, so he put her on the block list. He didn't want anything else to do with her. He talked to Reign a couple times to check on her, but he hadn't seen her. He couldn't blame her for being mad at him, so he was giving her some space. He was horny, so he finally reached out to Honey, and she was happy to kick it with him.

Nasir climbed out of the bed, then walked to the bathroom. He took a quick shower and brushed his teeth, then walked back into the bedroom. He put on a pair of basketball shorts, then climbed into bed. As soon as he closed his eyes, he heard a loud boom and then the sound of his alarm going off. He and Honey both jumped up from the bed. She wrapped a sheet around her naked frame, and he grabbed his gun off instinct.

They were running through the house, then his bedroom door was kicked open. Nasir was stood with his gun aimed, waiting on whoever was crazy enough to run up in his house.

"Freeze! Put your gun down now," a policer officer yelled. There were three more behind him with their guns aimed Nasir and Honey. "Nasir Stevens, you're under arrest for cocaine distribution and the manufacturing and distribution of a controlled substance. Anything you say, can will be held against you in the court of law."

Nasir bit down on the inside of his jaw while the officer placed the handcuffs on him. The officer pulled Nasir through the house, and he watched as they trashed his shit. Everything he and his grandmother worked hard for was being torn and broken up. He never thought he would be caught slipping. He had been careful since he started pushing major weight.

Nasir was dragged out to the police car. He sat there while they finished tearing up his crib looking for drugs and God knows what else. He didn't leave drugs in his house, so he wasn't worried about them finding anything. He watched Honey walk to her car and drive off. He sat and waited for about another fifteen minutes until they drove him to the station.

Nasir was fingerprinted, then taken to an interrogation room, where they made him sit and wait around for two hours until someone finally came in. When they came in and asked him questions, he denied everything and asked for his lawyer. The shit they were asking him let him know that someone had been running their mouth. After an hour of interrogation, he was able to make his phone call.

"What's up, bro? Are you good?" Blake asked on the first ring.

"Yeah. I don't have long. I have court at nine for a bail hearing. I need you to come to court and find out how much my bail is, then contact Reign. She has access to my money and accounts. Tell her how much my bail is and get the money out, then come bail me out.

"Okay, I got you," Blake said before hanging up.

Nasir was led to the back to a cell with a thin ass mattress. There was no way he could lay on that, because it would fuck his back up, so he decided to just sit on it. He leaned against the wall and closed his eyes until he fell asleep sitting up. As quickly as he closed his eyes, they were opening his cell ready to take him to court.

The judge set Nasir's bail for one hundred thousand dollars, so that meant he only had to pay ten thousand. He called Blake so that he could pay his bail and meet him at the county. He needed him to hurry up before he was processed, or he wouldn't be able to get out until that night. He was scheduled to return to court in two weeks, and he would have to tell them if he would take a plea deal or go to trial.

Nasir sat in lockup until about four when they announced he made bail. He grabbed his belongings, then walked out to the car, where Blake and Deja were waiting.

"Oh my God, Nas. Are you okay?" Deja asked.

"Yeah, I'm good. I have a meeting with my lawyer tomorrow, and we'll sit down and discuss things. Did you tell Reign that you were coming to pick me up?" Nasir inquired.

"Yeah. She said call her when you get home," Deja replied.

"How is the house? Did they fuck it up bad?" Nasir asked.

"The house overall is good, but all the furniture is fucked up. They cut the couches and took the TVs apart."

Nasir shook his head and sat back. The remainder of the drive to his house was quiet. Nas was lost in his thoughts, pondering what he should do.

Nasir walked in his house, and his eyes watered. They would have to throw everything away and start over. There were even a few holes in the wall. Since there was a big chance he was going to have to do time, he needed to sit down with his Blake and Deja to discuss the house because whenever he got out of jail, he would be moving on his own.

Nasir went to the bathroom and took a shower, then cleaned his bedroom as much as he could. Since he didn't get much sleep, he decided to go to sleep early so that he wouldn't be tired when he went to his lawyer's office.

The following morning, Nasir got dressed and headed to Oakbrook to meet up with his lawyer. His lawyer showed him all the evidence they had against him, and they had two informants, but they didn't give the names out. His lawyer told him he could either take a plea deal for six years and get out early for good behavior, or he could go to trial, but if he lost, he would be looking at twenty years. They had also added the gun he had to the charge since it wasn't registered, and he pointed it at the police, so either way he was doing time for something.

Nasir left the office and went home after the meeting. He packed a bag and headed to Faith's house. Since he was going to have to do some jail time, he wanted to spend as much time with his son as he could.

15

Reign walked in her house and couldn't control her smile. She was in pure bliss. Everything was going according to her plan. She was doing great in school, dance was going well, and she loved her house. It seemed like all the stress she was feeling over the last few months evaporated, and things were finally going her way.

She saw Sincere last week, and they had two amazing dates and mind-blowing sex to end the night. She hated when Sunday came around and she had to drop him off at the airport. It was getting harder and harder each time. Reign didn't know how long she would be able to just have sex with him and watch him leave. It was like every orgasm he gave her picked away at a piece of her heart.

Even though she told him she didn't want a relationship didn't mean it would stop her from falling for him. She had never been in love before, so she had nothing to compare it to. She didn't even know if she could call it love, but she did have strong feelings for him, stronger than she ever had for Jason and Nasir. Now that everything was falling into place for Reign, she felt now was a good time her to start therapy. She was about to start family therapy with her parents, but she debated on if she was ready to have her separate sessions as well.

Reign ran upstairs and put her duffel bag up. She had just come back from dancing at one of the basketball games. She hadn't heard from her mother since earlier, so she decided to check on her first. She turned the knob on her mother's door and immediately wished that she had knocked first.

"Why the hell are you two doing?" Reign yelled as she turned around to face the other way while her mother and father got dressed. She couldn't believe she had walked in on her parents having sex. She thought the days of seeing her mother naked were over. She was going to be scarred for life.

"Reign, I can explain," Nathaniel said.

"How can you explain this, Dad? You're married. How long has this been going on?" Reign asked.

"Today was the first time we actually had sex. Your mother had a great week at work, so I took her out to dinner to celebrate. We came back and were reminiscing. I think you know the rest after that," Nathaniel explained.

"I'm so sorry, Reign. You shouldn't have seen this. It was a mistake," Helen added.

Reign shook her head at how irresponsible her parents were being. She was the child, and they were fucking up more than her.

"I thought you said she'd be out for at least a few more hours," Nathaniel grumbled to Helen.

"It has been a few hours since we been here, Nate. You know you have the stamina of a racehorse," Helen replied.

"Ugh, you guys are so paying for my therapy," Reign mumbled.

Reign couldn't believe they were more concerned about why she was back early and not the fact that she knew they had sex.

"Can I go take a quick shower, then we sit down and talk about this," Helen asked.

"Yeah, me and Dad will be downstairs," Reign replied.

Reign walked downstairs and sat on the couch with her father behind her. They sat on the couch together. It was an awkward silence for a few minutes until Nathaniel spoke up.

"I'm sorry, Reign. I didn't know you were going to be here early. I know that's not an excuse, because me and your mother shouldn't be having sex since I'm married, but I guess old ways die hard."

"I understand that, Dad, but this can't happen again. I love both you and Mom, but I can't sit back and watch you break her again. She finally got the help she needed, and she's working on getting herself together. Right now is a sensitive time for her. The doctor at the rehab said the first year is the hardest, and she should only focus on staying sober and being productive. You're not going to leave Amelia, so it's time to let whatever feelings you have for my mom go and let her move on. When the time comes alone, she deserves to have someone that wants and loves her. I hope you understand," Reign told him.

"I'm so proud of you, baby girl. You're absolutely right. I had no business going there with your mother. We were just testing the waters, but it won't happen again," he assured her.

Reign and Nathaniel sat and talked until Helen came down a few minutes later in a pair of pajamas and her hair pulled back. Reign couldn't blame her father for still being attracted to her mother, because Helen looked good as hell, even dressed down.

"Let me start off by saying what happened tonight wasn't planned. The past two months while I was in rehab, your father was the only person I talked to and I allowed to visit me. I wasn't mad at you because you allowed him back in your life. I didn't want you to see me go through that process. Some days, I was mad and depressed. You had already seen me at my low more times than you should have. I wanted you to be able to work on yourself without worrying about me too. During that time, I got a glimpse of the old Nathaniel. I'm older though now, and I know my worth. I would never to be a mistress or side bitch again. You don't have to worry about me relapsing. I'll find someone to settle down with later. Right now, I just want to be by myself," Helen explained.

"I'm glad you told me this, Ma. I thought you didn't want to talk to or see me because of Dad."

"No, baby. I understood why you didn't tell me you were building a relationship with him. With the way my mindset was back then, I wouldn't have told myself either."

"Well, you two don't have to worry about me saying anything, and if you do decide to cross this line again, please don't let me see it. This puts me in an uncomfortable position when it comes to Mason, Amelia, and Iris," Reign said.

"I know. It's just things aren't good at home right now, Reign, but I'm going to make all this right," Nathaniel added.

"Okay. I'm going to give you two some time to talk. I need to get my stuff together for tomorrow. I'll see y'all later." Reign stood from the couch and kissed both her parents on the cheek before heading upstairs to her bedroom.

Reign took a shower in her bathroom, then put on a pair of pajama pants and a top. She grabbed her blunt and phone, then sat outside on her patio. Her parents had ruined her great mood. She just hoped they knew what they were doing because she didn't want it to affect her relationship with her siblings.

Reign was enjoying the breeze when her phone started to ring. She looked down at it and saw it was Nasir. She hadn't seen him since she moved out of his house. She talked to him on the phone almost every day, but that was about it.

"Hello," Reign answered.

"Hey. What are you doing?"

"Nothing, at home chilling. What's up?"

"Can I come over? You know I'm going to turn myself in tomorrow. I just want to spend my last night with you," Nasir said.

"Okay. I'll text you my address. Don't take all night, or I won't open the door for you," Reign warned him before hanging up.

Nasir walked in his son's room and kissed him on the forehead, then walked to Faith's room. He grabbed his wallet and keys, then headed toward the front of her apartment.

"You're about to go?" Faith asked.

"Yeah. I have some things to take care of tonight before I turn myself in tomorrow."

"Will you be back tonight? I thought that we could spend your last night together," Faith pouted.

"Faith, I just spent the last two weeks here with you and my son. I can't stay tonight. I have to meet up with Reign to take care of some things before I turn myself in tomorrow. Reign will give you money once a month for my son," Nasir replied.

"Why the fuck are you meeting up with Reign? I thought you didn't fuck with her like that. Now you're telling me she's the one sending that'll be sending me money for our son every month. You know I don't fuck that bitch like that," Faith snapped.

"I never said I didn't fuck with her anymore. I told you we were taking a break. That doesn't mean I cut ties with her. And believe me, she doesn't fuck with you either, but if you want the money, she'll be the one sending it to you unless you plan on taking care of him on your own."

"I swear I can't stand your dumb ass sometimes. That girl broke your heart, and you came running to me, and now you're just going to trust her with everything, and it's fuck me again," Faith cried.

Nasir didn't have time to entertain Faith, because if he was late, he knew Reign wouldn't let him in, so he ignored her and left the house.

Nas drove the twenty minutes to Reign's house and parked in the front. He climbed out the car and walked up to her front door. He rang the bell and waited for someone to answer. After waiting about a minute, the door opened, and he was face-to-face when Nathaniel.

"Hey, Nas. What are you doing here?" Nathaniel asked.

"I texted Reign and asked her could I come over so that we could talk," Nas replied.

"Okay. I don't know what's going on between you and my daughter, but don't come over here starting no shit."

"I'm not. I'm turning myself in tomorrow and just wanted to spend some time with Reign before then."

"Alright. Her room is upstairs on the third floor. Turn right and go to the end of the hall."

Nasir walked past Nathaniel and walked upstairs. He stopped on the second floor and did a double take when he saw Helen cleaning up. Reign told him her mom was out of rehab, but he didn't expect her to look that good.

"Hey, Helen. How are you doing?" Nasir spoke.

"Hey, Nasir. I'm doing good. How are you?"

"I'm okay. I just stopped by to see Reign."

"Alright. Before you go up there, I want to thank you for looking out for Reign when I wasn't well enough to do so. I appreciate that," Helen told him.

"You're welcome, but there's no thanks needed. Reign was my girl, and I did what I had to do," Nasir said.

Nasir walked upstairs and knocked on Reign's bedroom door until he heard her tell him to come in.

Nasir walked into the room and looked around. He was impressed with how good her place looked. Nathaniel went all out for Reign and Helen. He sat on the couch Reign had in the corner of her room. She climbed from her bed and sat next to him.

"Hey. How are you feeling with everything going on?" Reign asked.

"I'm doing okay. I'm content with the decision I made. I know I don't have anything to worry about with you, Deja, and Blake taking care of everything for me."

Blake was going to work with Ricky while Nasir was locked up, and Deja would help out with the accountant part of everything. He put Reign's name on his bank accounts and gave her the combination to his safe so she would have access to his funds. She was going to also collect his money from Ricky once a month, as well as the money for Mason since she was the only one both of them trusted. Ricky thought Nasir was crazy leaving Reign in charge of his money, but he wasn't worried about her stealing it. He was giving her a thousand dollars a month just for collecting his money, sending money to Faith, and putting money on his books.

"I know we haven't been on the best of terms, but I wouldn't have wished this upon you. I really do still care about you, Nasir, and no matter what happens, we can work on being friends. I'll make sure your money is put away and kept safe. You don't have to worry about me fucking you over," Reign said.

"I'm not worried about you fucking me over. If I thought that was even an option, I wouldn't have put your name on everything," Nasir told her.

"Why don't you go take a shower, then we can climb in bed and watch a movie?" Reign suggested. Since it was Nasir's last night out, she wanted to spend it like they used to.

Nasir got up from the couch and went into Reign's bathroom. He took a quick shower and brushed his teeth, then walked back into her bedroom. He grabbed a pair of boxers from his bag and slipped them on before climbing in bed next to her.

Nasir kept stealing glances over at Reign while she searched for a movie. After flipping for what seemed like forever, she stopped on *Money Talks*. It was a movie that they both enjoyed.

Reign laid her head on Nasir's chest and he wrapped his arm around her. They remained like that for the remainder of the movie. It felt good to have Reign in his arms. He didn't think he was going to get the chance to do it again. He wished it was under better circumstances, but he would take what he could get.

Once the movie was off, Reign turned to Pandora and allowed music to play. She looked him in the eyes, and he couldn't tell if she was waiting on him to make a move or what. He didn't want to get cursed out, but at the same time, he couldn't resist, so he leaned in and kissed her. When she didn't stop him, he kissed her deeper, then next thing she knew, they were naked, making love in her bed. He made sure to take his time so they both would remember that night. They made love into the middle of the night and passed out in each other's arms.

The following morning, Reign and Nasir showered, then got dressed. They had a quick breakfast before she took him to the courthouse. She couldn't stay for his court appearance since she had class, but it wasn't like they didn't already know what the outcome would be.

"I'm going to miss you Reign. I don't expect you to wait around for me. All I ask is for a fair chance when I come home. I think me being gone will give me time to reflect on everything as well as give you enough time to think about what it is that you want."

"You don't have to worry about me getting serious with anyone while you're gone. I told you I plan on finishing up school first, so we can play everything by ear. You just try not to get in any trouble so that you don't have to stay longer then needed."

"I promise to be on my best behavior. I love you, Reign, and nothing will change that."

Nasir leaned over and kissed Reign on the lips, then climbed out of the car. He took a deep breath before going in the courthouse to meet his demise. He stopped in the hallway when he saw Faith and his son. He picked his son up and kissed him all over the face before giving him back to Faith.

"I'm sorry for starting a fight with you, Nas. It's just that I'm going to miss you, and I found out that I'm pregnant," Faith told him.

"What? You need to get rid of it, Faith. How are you going to take care of two kids on your own? I'll have Reign send you extra money for an abortion."

"Fuck you, Nasir. Give me my damn son. You don't have to worry about us while you're locked up, you selfish son of a bitch," Faith screamed, causing a scene.

Nasir shook his head, then walked away to find his brother, sister, and lawyer. He was going to miss his son, but he wouldn't miss having to deal with Faith's bullshit.

❧ 16 ❧

FOUR YEARS LATER

Sincere sat on the edge of the bed with his face in the palm of his hands. He needed to leave so that he could catch his flight, but he needed to talk to Destiny before he left. He looked at his watch again and sighed. Of all the times for Destiny to be late, she chose that day. He waited five more minutes before she finally walked in.

"Hey, baby. You wanted to see me before you left." Destiny smiled.

"Yeah, I did. What the hell is this Destiny?" Nasir asked, picking up the papers and handing them to her. It was papers from Planned Parenthood. She got an abortion two months ago and didn't tell him about it.

"I'm sorry, Sin. I didn't know how to tell you," Destiny cried.

"You didn't know how to tell me that you killed my fucking child, or you didn't know how to tell me that it probably wasn't mine?" Sincere asked.

"I didn't know if it was yours, Sin, and I knew that if it wasn't, you would leave me. Plus, I'm a first-year resident. Right now is not the time for me to have a baby," Destiny said.

"Destiny, you know how bad I wanted a baby, and you agreed on having one with me. If you didn't want one yet, you should have said something before, and I wouldn't have nutted in you. We could've continued using protection. You know if that baby was mine, I would have helped you take care of it while you worked. You should have waited to have a paternity test done."

"I couldn't do that, because then if it came back that you weren't the father, I'd be without a husband and raising a baby that I didn't want."

"Well, you should have thought about that before you decided on starting an affair with your co-worker. I tried to forgive you for that, and I stopped the preparation for our divorce, but I can't forgive you for this. If you had to question the paternity, that means you slept with him again after I found out about your affair because we went to the doctor, and everything came back negative, including the pregnancy test. I'm going to talk to my lawyer and have him to start back with the proceedings of our divorce. I think I'm going to take my stepfather up on his offer and move to Chicago to help out with his new office."

"You can't move back to Chicago. I'm in the first year of my residency. If I leave now, I'll be a year behind, and ain't no telling if there's any openings in Chicago at a good hospital. I uprooted everything and finished med school down here. I fought to find an internship last minute and got accepted in a residency," Destiny snapped.

"If you wanted to be here with me so much, then you wouldn't have started fucking somebody else."

"Oh, please. I just did what you didn't have the nerves to do. We both know that you don't want to be here with me. You just needed an out that didn't make you look like the bad guy. You still have feelings for that bitch Reign, and you settled with me since she wasn't ready for you yet," Destiny pointed out.

"If you thought all of this was true, why the fuck would you agree to marry me then? You know what? It doesn't' even matter anymore, because we're done. Just sign the papers, Destiny, and we can get this over as soon as possible. I'll make arrangements to get my things moved out. You can have this house," Sincere told her.

Sincere stood from the bed and grabbed his two suitcases that he packed. He packed most of the important things he was going to need since he didn't know when he'd be coming back to Memphis.

"So after everything that happened, you're still about to go leave for Chicago like we don't have unfinished business? I think you should stay so that we can talk about this," Destiny said.

"I can't stand to look at your ass right now. As far as I'm concerned, I've said everything that needs to be said. You should have been talking to me before all of this shit started. If you weren't happy, you should have said something."

"It's not that, Sincere. I am happy with you. Our schedules have been crazy. You work all day, and I work all night. We were never seeing each other, and I was lonely. Alex and I had late-night study sessions and shifts together, so it just happened. You have to believe me when I say he doesn't mean anything to me. We're just friends. I haven't touched him since I had the abortion."

"Destiny, do you hear yourself? You had the abortion two months ago. That was four months after I found out about your affair. I have to go," Sincere said before walking out. He walked to the car that was waiting for him, and he put his bags in the trunk and sat in the back seat. His mind instantly went to the words that Destiny said. He'd only been with her because Reign wasn't ready, which was partly true.

Reign and Sincere fucked around for about a year after she told him they couldn't be together. He continued seeing her because he had hopes that he could change her mind, but she wasn't budging. His feelings for her were too strong for them to keep going about things the way they were, so they agreed to just be friends with no sex involved. Three months after that, he started back dating Destiny, and she agreed to move to Memphis to be with him.

Things were going great, so a year later he proposed to her. Since Destiny was in the middle of her internship, they decided to elope two weeks later at city hall. They agreed to work on having a baby after she finished her internship, so he couldn't understand what was going through her head. If he knew they weren't on the same page, he never would have married her.

Sincere and Reign still talked every now and then, but it wasn't like it used to be between them and he hadn't seen her in over a year. Once he married Destiny, it was hard for him to look Reign in the eyes. He didn't know how to tell her that he was married to another woman. Even though they were never together, it felt wrong to him because Reign should have been the one he was married to, not Destiny. It was crazy how their marriage barely lasted two years, and they were already calling it quits.

Sincere looked on the bright side of things. Now that he was ending things with Destiny and Reign graduated college, he was ready to make Reign his woman. Neither of them had an excuse to not be together, and he wouldn't be taking no for an answer this time.

Sincere got dropped off at the airport and checked in right before it was time for his plane to take off. Had he been five minutes later, he would have missed his flight. He slept during the entire flight. Once he landed in Chicago, he took a taxi to his house. He dropped his things off, then got in his car and drove to Reign's house. He should have called first, but his nerves were on edge, so he was just going with the flow.

☙❦☙

Reign was laying in bed in a pair of boy shorts and a sports bra. For the first time in a while, she didn't have anything to do, so she was chilling in bed, watching movies, and eating snacks. She would have called Jason to come over, but he was babysitting

Eve's daughter while she worked. She loved her goddaughter, but she wasn't in the mood to chase her around.

Halfway through the movie, her phone stated to ring. She looked down at it and saw it was Sincere. She smiled when she saw his name. It was crazy how she still got butterflies whenever she talked to him, and he hadn't touched her in three years.

"Hello," Reign answered.

"What you up to?" Sincere asked.

"Laying here watching *Selena*. What are you doing?" Reign asked.

"Waiting for you to come open your door," Sincere said.

"The lies you tell. You know you're not at my house." Reign laughed.

"I am though, so come open the door," Sincere told her.

Reign jumped up from her bed and put her snacks away, then walked downstairs. She looked in the mirror and straightened her hair out before opening the door for him.

"What are you doing here?" Reign inquired.

"I missed you," Sincere confessed.

"I missed you too." Reign smiled.

Reign grabbed Sincere by his arm and led him up to her bedroom. As soon as the door was closed, Sincere pushed Reign against it and crashed his lips into hers. He went over there to talk to her first, but seeing her in just boy shorts and a sports bra, he couldn't resist.

Reign and Sincere stripped out of their clothes. She dropped to her knees in front of him and gripped his dick. She stroked him slowly before placing him in her mouth. She licked the head, where precum had formed.

"Fuck, Reign." He gripped the back of her hair, and she grinned before taking him back in her mouth. She flattened her tongue and began sucking him off. His hips lifted and began pounding in her mouth until he stiffened and came down her throat.

Sincere lay on the bed and pulled Reign down with him.

"I want you get on top and ride my face."

Sincere didn't have to tell Reign more than once. She straddled his face. He immediately shoved his tongue inside her and held on to both of her thighs tightly. She gripped the headboard as she rode his face.

"Oh my God. This feels so good," Reign cried as she picked up the pace. Sincere shoved two fingers inside her, and it drove her over the edge, making her cum on his face.

"Damn, I missed you. You taste amazing," Sincere said.

Reign climbed off of Sincere's face and slid down on his erect dick. A moan escaped both of their mouths as her pussy clenched his dick. A tear rolled down Reign's cheek as she rode Sincere slowly. She didn't realize how much she missed him. She spent the last few years sleeping with Jason, and she even fucked Tavian a couple times, but neither of them could compare to Sincere in the bedroom.

"I'm about to cum," Reign moaned.

"Well, come on this dick then," Sincere demanded.

Sincere waited for Reign to ride her orgasm out, then he flipped her over onto her back and entered her. He spread her legs wide open and deep stroked her pussy, making sure to hit her spot every time. The only thing that could be heard through the room was the sounds of their pleasure.

"Oh fuck, baby... Please don't stop," Reign cried as she dug her nails in his back. She clenched her pussy around him tightly until she was squirting all over his dick.

"Shit, Reign," he growled, rubbing her clit and slamming into her until she came again. He loved how her body still reacted to his.

Sincere pulled out of Reign, and she rolled over on all fours. He slid back inside of her without warning.

"Yesss. I missed this dick so much, Sin. Please don't leave me again," Reign begged as she threw her pussy back on him.

"This is your dick, baby. You don't have to worry about that. Who this pussy belongs to?"

"It's yours, baby," Reign cried out.

Sincere grabbed a handful of Reign's hair and fucked her harder until she was squirting again.

"Tell me you'll be my woman now," Sincere demanded.

"Yes, I'll be with you, Sin. Oh, God. Damn, Sincere... What are you doing to me?" she screamed.

"I'm making up for lost time, baby. You gon' let me fuck this pussy all night?" Sincere asked.

"Yes, daddy. You can have it whatever way you want," Reign moaned out.

Sincere picked up the pace and fucked Reign harder until he felt himself dropping his load inside of her.

"I missed you so fucking much, Reign. I was serious about you wanting to be my girl now, Reign. We can't go back to the way things used to be. I love you too much for that," Sincere confessed.

"I don't want to go back to how things were either. I'm ready to be with you as well. I love you, Sincere. I have for a while," Reign admitted with a smile.

Sincere leaned over and kissed Reign on the lips. He didn't think he would ever see the day that she admitted she loved him or that they would ever finally be together.

"I just want you to know even though we didn't talk all the time, that didn't mean you weren't on my mind. I just had some things I was dealing with and trying to figure out. I knew that if I saw you, it would make things difficult for both of us. I wanted to respect your wishes and give you the time you needed to finish school. Now that you're done and I'm back, I hope you have everything out of your system because I'm not willing to share you, Reign."

"I'm not willing to share you either, so I hope whoever it was that had your attention these past three years is out of your system because I'm not having a relationship with you like I did with Nasir," Reign told him.

"You don't have to worry about anyone. It's always been

about you, Reign, even when she was in the picture. I know I showed up today out of the blue, so that means you haven't had a chance to call things off with whoever you were dealing with, but I expect you to do that tomorrow," Sincere replied.

"I mean, I wasn't in anything serious. I slept with someone every now and then, but we weren't serious, and he already knows that we never would be, but if it makes you feel better, I'll let him know that I'm with you."

"Okay, and what about your ex?" Sincere asked.

"He's in prison, Sincere, so I doubt you have anything to worry about with him. I talk to him once a week and take care of business for him."

"Does he think two are still together?"

"No. I broke up with him a few weeks before he went to jail. We chose to remain friends, and I look out for him while he was away. It's the least I could do after everything he did for me. I don't have feelings for him anymore, and you don't have to worry about me trying to be with him when he comes home. I'm not going to lie; I was confused at first about which one of y'all I wanted, but after going without seeing either of you, my heart gravitated toward you more. I think it was just I liked the idea of being with him because he had been there for me at my worst."

Sincere and Reign stayed up and talked, then made love again until they both passed out in pure bliss.

❧ 17 ❧

Reign was standing at the sink, loading the dishwasher when she felt a strong pair of arms wrap around her. She smiled, then turned her head and wrapped her arms around Sincere. For the past two days, they had been locked away in her house in their own personal bubble watching TV, making love, and catching up like old times.

"You're dressed. Does that mean you're about to leave me now?" Reign asked.

"Yes. I have to go meet up with my parents to discuss some things and go home to change clothes." Sincere had a gym bag in his car with a set of clean clothes, even though he didn't need them while he was at Reign's house since they were pretty much naked the entire time since it was only them two at the house.

"I don't want you to leave me. I just got you back." Reign pouted.

"Baby, I'll be back this evening to spend time with you. You don't have to worry about me leaving you. I'm moving back here for good. I'll just go to Memphis for meetings when needed. When is your roommate coming back?" Sincere asked, referring to Kehlani.

"She'll be back in a few hours," Reign replied.

"I guess that means we're going to have to keep our sessions in the bedroom," Sincere stated before kissing Reign's lips.

"Nah. We can still have fun in other places. You're just going to have to keep it down." Reign laughed.

"Girl, you know that be you." Sincere chuckled.

"Whatever. Hurry up so you can come back. I have a meeting to get ready for anyway," Reign replied.

Sincere gave Reign one final kiss, then left out and headed to his house. He parked in his driveway since he was leaving right back out, then went inside the house. He walked to the kitchen and found Silas sitting at the counter eating.

"Aye, man. What's going on? Your mama and everybody been looking for you. I tried to cover for you the best I could. Why don't you have your phone on?" Silas asked.

"I turned it off when I got to Reign's house. I had a lot of things to discuss with her, and I didn't want to be interrupted. I'm about to go to my mom's house in a minute though because I need to talk to Arnez about his job offer," Sin replied.

"You're about to move back? What about Destiny?"

"Man, I'm done with her. She was still cheating, and then she got an abortion without telling me."

"Damn. I'm sorry, man. That's fucked up. You know how I felt about that girl anyway. I like Reign better. You know your mom family gon' give you a hard time, but I got your back. You need to call Pops though and let him know what you plan on doing."

"I already talked to him when I was at the airport before I got out here. He's cool with whatever decision I make. I'm grown, so at the end of the day, it's about what I want. I'm not about to be with a bitch that keeps cheating on me, especially when I love another woman anyway."

Sincere and Silas sat and talked for a few more minutes, then Sin changed his clothes and left back out of the house. He powered his phone on and drove to his mom's house. His phone was barely on for a minute when it started ringing. He sighed when he saw Destiny's name come across his screen.

"Yeah?" Sincere answered.

"Why the fuck hasn't anyone heard from you in two days? Your family didn't even know you were in town."

"I had some business to take care of, and Silas knew I was here," Sincere replied.

"Silas doesn't count. You know I don't like him."

"I don't give a damn if you like him or not. That's still my brother, so be careful what you say next."

"Whatever. You couldn't wait to run to that bitch, huh," Destiny seethed.

"What I do is no longer your concern. Just make it easy for both of us and sign the damn papers. I know you have them by now," Sincere yelled.

"I'm not signing shit so you can run off and be with that green-eyed bitch. You gon' have to fight me in court," Destiny snapped.

"I don't have a problem with that. Just remember you signed a prenup agreement, so if you take me to court, I'll make sure you don't get shit, including my house that you're living in," Sincere pointed out.

"Damn. You like the ho that much that you're willing to leave me homeless?" Destiny cried.

"It's up to you, Des. I'm trying to go the easy route, and you're making this harder than it has to be. You're the one that fucked up, not me. Just sign the papers, and we'll be good."

"Fuck you, Sincere. You already know your family and my daddy won't be happy about this."

"Girl, I don't give a fuck who ain't happy about my decisions. I got to go. Don't contact me unless you signed the papers." Sincere hung up the phone and parked in his parents' driveway.

Sincere walked up to his parents' house and rang the doorbell. He waited a couple minutes until the door was swung open.

"Sincere, where have you been? We've been worried sick about you," Sincere's mother, Lorraine, said.

"I had some things to take care of before I came over here. Is Arnez here?"

"Yeah. He's in the living room," Lorraine replied.

Sincere walked into the living room and shook his stepfather's hand before sitting down across from him.

"Hey, Sincere. What brings you here?" Arnez asked.

"I'm going to take you up on your job offer and come help Ace out here," Sincere told him.

"That's great, but what about your company and wife in Memphis?"

"I'll still have my company in Memphis. I have someone there to take care of it, and I'll Zoom in on meetings. I'm going to start another label out here once I find an office. As far as my wife goes, we're getting a divorce," Sincere replied.

"So it is true. You're leaving my best friend for another woman," Andrea yelled, walking in the living room interrupting their conversation.

"It's not like that ,but I am going to be with someone else," Sincere admitted.

"Sincere, you know we don't believe in divorces and adultery. You need to leave whatever woman you've been seeing alone and go back home to your wife," Lorraine added.

"With all due respect, Ma, I love you, but this is my decision. I'm not divorcing her because I cheated or because of another woman. I'm divorcing her because she cheated, and I forgave her, but then I found out the affair never ended, and she got an abortion, so no, I won't sit around and wait to see what happens next. I won't pretend like I'm okay with that and can forgive her," Sincere fumed.

"Sincere, everyone makes mistakes, son. Marriage is supposed to be for better or worse," Lorraine pointed out.

"Look, Ma, I've made my decision, and there's nothing you or anyone can say to change that. I'm not in love with Destiny anyway. I never should have married her. I thought we had the same goals, but I was wrong. It is what it is though. I'm going to be with the person that I love, whether any of you like it or not."

"I'm letting you know right now. I'm not approving of a new relationship, Sincere. Destiny will always be my only daughter-in-law unless Ace gets married," Lorraine said.

"Well, it's a good thing I'm twenty-six years old and don't need your or anybody else's approval."

"Okay, why don't we all just calm down and discuss this another time?" Arnez reasoned.

"I'm not discussing this again. I said what I needed to say. If you still want my help, let me know. If not, I understand. I'll just focus on my companies." Sincere shrugged.

"I can't believe you would leave my friend for a mistake after everything you put her through. She left her entire life here for you," Andrea reminded him.

"Mind your business, Andrea. I didn't do anything to her since we got back together. I tried, but this time, it's all on her. Just be a good friend and tell her to sign the divorce papers before she ends up homeless." Sincere stood from the couch and left the house. He refused to let his family mess up his good mood. He didn't know how long Reign's meeting was going to be, so he was going to go back to his house a do some work for a few hours before going back to hers.

Reign stuck her lasagna in the oven, then went to join her girls in the living room. When she got back from her meeting, Kehlani was already at the house, so she decided to invite Eve and Ava over as well so she could catch them up on everything that had been going on with her since she'd been MIA over the last couple days.

"So ladies, I called you over here because I have some news," Reign announced.

"What's up? It better be good since you haven't replied to none of my messages," Ava said.

"Shit, she hasn't replied to mine either, and I'm her roommate," Kehlani pointed out.

"I'm sorry. Y'all know how I get when I'm trying to figure things out. But anyway, I went to my meeting today, and it was great. As you all know, I got the building I wanted for my studio and store. I talked to the contractors today, and everything should be ready and remodeled in about two months. I'm going to have a grand opening a couple weeks after that."

"Congratulations," the girls said simultaneously.

"Thank you, but that's not all. Sincere came over Saturday night, and I've decided to finally give him a chance." Reign smiled.

"Bitch, I knew you was glowing for a reason. You know I'm team Sin, so I'm here for it." Kehlani beamed.

"What about your ex? Doesn't he come home in a few months?" Ava asked.

"What about him? Nasir and I are just friends. He's been gone four years now. I only talk to him once a week, if that," Reign replied.

"Fuck her ex. What about my brother? He's been by your side the last few years, and you're just going to drop him because Sin decided to come back? You're not thinking clear right now. You told me that you couldn't be with Sin because you didn't want to be in a long-distance relationship," Eve pointed out.

Eve found out about Jason and Reign last year when she showed up at Reign's house unannounced while Jason was there. They didn't feel the need to hide it since Reign was grown now, so they decided to tell Eve everything. At first, Eve was pissed at them for keeping it from her, but eventually, she came around to the idea of them being together.

"Eve, chill. You always on some hating shit. That's your girl. You should be happy for her," Kehlani interjected.

"Fuck that. I'm her real friend that's been here since day one, so it's my job to keep it real with her and not just tell her what makes her feel good. I'm not here to use her and pacify her," Eve shouted.

"Bitch, I'm getting really tired of your shady ass. You gon' make me beat your motherfucking ass like your nigga do. Ain't nobody using her. You just mad that she let me move in here with her and not you. I'm not living off of her. I give her money every fucking month, and I'm a real friend to her. It doesn't matter if I haven't known her the longest. I don't throw shit back in her face or remind her of her past. It was all good when she needed you, but when she got her shit together, your ass turned fake," Kehlani snapped.

Reign sighed as she listened to her friends argue. It was something those two did on the regular, but Kehlani was speaking nothing but the truth. That's why Reign didn't jump in to stop her this time. Ever since Reign let Kehlani move in last year, Eve had been acting shadier than normal.

Eve waited until Reign told her Kehlani was moving in to say that she wanted to move in with her. By then, it was too late because Reign wasn't giving up her guest room, and her house wasn't equipped for a toddler. Besides that, Eve was still with Ricky, and she didn't need him at her house all the time in her business. It was bad enough she had to deal with him to get Nasir's money still. She couldn't wait until Nas came home so she could close that chapter in her life.

If Eve really needed a place to live, then Reign would've budged temporarily, but Eve had a two-bedroom apartment for her and her daughter already, so she didn't know why she was acting like that when she knew Kehlani didn't have anywhere to live once she graduated.

Reign didn't want to be alone after Helen moved out, so it worked out for both of them. Once Kehlani got a stable job, she gave Reign fifteen hundred dollars a month because she wasn't comfortable living off of Reign and her father. Reign loved sharing a place with Kehlani, but she missed living with her mother as well.

Helen started dating an investment banker from her job three years ago. They instantly hit it off. They dated for about a year before they got engaged. They had a small wedding six months after that, and Helen moved out. It was a bittersweet moment for Reign when her mother told her that she was engaged because she knew that meant she was going to leave her. She was sad about that because they had finally built the bond she was looking for, but she couldn't be selfish when it came to her mother. She had never seen Helen so happy in her life, and she couldn't take that away from her. She was now grown, and it was time for her to grow up.

"Aye, y'all don't even have to do all this. We're supposed to be popping a bottle right now and celebrating with our girl. Reign is a grown woman and can make her own decisions. If she wants to be with Sincere and he makes her happy, then it's our job, as her friends, to be there for her. If it doesn't work out with them, it's still our job, as her friends, to be there for her. I get it, Eve. Jason is your brother, so your loyalty lays with him, but we all know he ain't shit. What he and Reign have is fun. They were never serious about each other and would never been in a real relationship. As her friend, you shouldn't want her to settle for Jason," Ava spoke up, interrupting Reign's thoughts. Reign was shocked to hear Ava say something because, usually, Ava sat back and was quiet whenever Eve and Kehlani went at it, mainly because she was new to the group and didn't know the full details of everything that went on between them.

Reign met Ava two years ago at her job. She started off as Ava's dance instructor, and one day, Ava asked her out to drinks after practice. Reign didn't have any plans, so she agreed to go. They got to talking, and Reign found out Ava was a single mother and looking for a part-time job. There was an opening at Reign's job for a receptionist, so Reign put in a good word for her. Once she was hired, they hung out more. Eventually, Reign introduced her to Kehlani and Eve. Ever since then, they all were cool.

"Okay, it's enough of the bullshit. If y'all not about to box it out, let's eat and pop this bottle until my man gets here. I love and appreciate all three of you ladies, but right now, I need my friends, not a mother. You all know I don't just jump into shit, so this has to have been something that I had already given some thoughts too. I can't live my life in fear hoping that Sincere doesn't put me through what Nasir did. Sin isn't Nas and unlike Nas I know Sin loves me for real and I love him. We're not doing a long-distance relationship either. He's moving out here to Chicago for good. This is finally my chance to see if Sin is the one for me. If not, then I can say at least I tried. So I need all of my girls to be happy for me. I want good vibes only," Reign told them.

Eve and Kehlani apologized to Reign for arguing and ruining the moment. The remainder of the evening went smoothly. The girls ate and drank until Sin showed up. Once he got there, the girls said their goodbyes. Ava and Eve left to go home, and Kehlani went to her room so the couple could have some alone time.

✺ 18 ✺

Reign was sitting in front of her mirror, brushing her hair into a ponytail. She had just got in from work and was tired. She loved her job at the studio, but she would be glad when her dance studio and store was open so she could work her own schedule. She busted her ass over the last few years with school and work. Now she was ready for it all to pay off.

Reign got up and went into her bathroom to take a shower. She closed her eyes and allowed the hot water to cascade over her body. Fifteen minutes passed before she decided to climb out of the shower. She moisturized her body, then put on one of her nightshirts and slides before going downstairs so she could find something to eat for dinner. By the time she made it to the kitchen, the doorbell went off. She wasn't expecting anyone, but she was curious who was at her door, so she hurriedly went downstairs and looked through the peephole. She opened the door and smiled broadly.

"What are you doing here?" Reign asked.

"Well, that wasn't the greeting I was expecting," Sincere replied.

"I'm sorry, baby. I'm just surprised to see you here," Reign
said.

"I know. I wanted to surprise you. I finished up work early
today, so I had time to go to the grocery store to grab some
things so that I could cook dinner for you."

"What? Are you serious?"

"Yeah, so come on," Sincere said.

Reign closed and locked her door, then followed Sincere
upstairs to her kitchen. She sat on the stool at the island while
Sin removed everything from the bags. Sincere washed his
hands, then got started on dinner while Reign sat pretty and
watched him. They made small talk in between to pass time. He
was making spaghetti, catfish, and garlic bread.

"Come over and let me know if anything else needs to be
added to this sauce." Reign got up and walked over to where Sin
was and tasted the spaghetti sauce.

"This is good." Reign looked up at Sin, licking her lips.

"Hmmm, let me taste." Sincere put his hand around Reign's
waist and pulled her in for a kiss. Reign wrapped her arms
around his neck and deepened the kiss. He slid his hand down
her body and gripped a handful of her ass. He moved to her
neck, leaving a soft trail of kisses. He lifted her dress, then
picked her up and sat her on the counter. He sat on the stool in
front of her and dove in headfirst. He ate her out until her legs
started to shake and she was cumming in his mouth.

Sincere lifted Reign from the island, then turned her around
and bent her over it. He stood up and released his member from
his jeans. He held on to her waist and slid inside of her. He
grabbed a handful of her hair and thrust in and out of her fast.
She bit down on her bottom lip as she gripped the counter.

"Fucckkk... Right there, baby," Reign cried out.

Sincere smacked her ass and pulled her head back as he deep
stroked her, picking up the pace.

"I'm about to cum, baby. You gon' cum again for me?" Sincere
grunted.

He reached around and played in Reign's wetness, making her clench her walls around his dick, causing her to cum with him.

"Damn, baby. I need you to come over and cook for me all the time if this comes with it." Reign smiled.

"Well, if you moved in with me, you could have in-house dick at your disposal," Sincere told her.

"Is that your way of asking me to move in with you?" Reign inquired.

"If your answer is yes, then I'm asking. You said your lease is up in three months and you had to decide on what you wanted to do. Why go through the process of finding a house or renewing this lease again when you could just stay with me?" Sincere fixed his clothes, then got back to cooking.

"I don't know, Sincere. We just got together. I'm not trying to rush things."

"Reign, it's not like we just met. We've known each other over five years. I love you, and you love me. We've been through the dating process and 'getting to know each other' stage already. I'm not trying to start over. I told you I see you in my future, and you're a part of my long-term goals. I'm hoping I'm a part of yours too," Sincere said.

"You are a part of my long-term goals. I can't see me spending my life with anybody else. You helped me, even when I couldn't help myself, and for that, I'll be forever grateful. Let me run a few things by Kehlani and make sure she's on track to getting her own place, then we can discuss this again," Reign replied.

"Well, it's not a no, so I can work with that."

Reign and Sincere continued to talk until he was finished cooking. He made their plates, and they sat down to have dinner. Once they finished eating, they showered and watched a movie until they fell asleep.

Nasir paced the floor back and forth. He had been trying to contact Reign for the past couple days, but she wasn't answering her phone. He wanted to make sure everything was good with her, so he dialed Eve's number instead to see what's up.

Nasir said his name, then waited while the operator talked before Eve accepted the call.

"What's up, big bro," Eve answered.

"Hey, sis. What's up with your girl? I've been trying to call her the past few days, and she not answering," Nasir replied.

"Honestly, I haven't talked to her in a few days either. I fell back some because I'm not feeling some decisions she made," Eve stated.

Hearing that piqued Nasir's interest. Now he really needed to know what was going on.

"What decisions are you talking about? What happened?"

"Let's just say I don't like how she's being naïve about the company she's keeping," Eve stated.

"Come on now, Eve. You're talking in circles. Just tell me what's going on. You know if you don't, Ricky will because I know you told him."

"Fine, but you better not tell Reign I told you. You have me going against the girl code," Eve said.

"Okay. I won't say nothing," Nasir told her.

"Reign has that bitch Kehlani living with her now, and she's a bad influence. Not only that, but Reign is in a relationship with the dude that you caught her up with. I know Ricky told you about her and Jason. She used my brother like she used you until she didn't need either of you anymore," Eve snapped.

Nasir didn't care about nothing Eve said until she mentioned the word *relationship*. He was naïve to believe Reign would be celibate for four years. Reign had actually told Nasir about her and Jason on her own because that was the kind of person she was. She didn't hide things or try to cover her tracks, so that meant things was fresh with her and dude. He just hated that she wasn't accepting his calls, but he had a trick for her.

"Okay, good looking out. I'll talk to you later," Nasir said before hanging up the phone. He and Eve weren't friends, so he didn't have anything to talk to her about. He just used her to get information about Reign.

After the conversation Nasir had with Eve, he was in a foul mood. He didn't have that much time left, so he didn't want to get in trouble for going off on someone, so he went back to his cell. The only time he left out was to have dinner, then he went back.

Nasir grabbed his notepad and pencil, then sat on his bed. He liked drawing when he was in high school, but once he started slanging dope, he stopped. Since there wasn't much to do in jail, he started back doing it and perfected his craft. He didn't watch much TV while there, because he didn't like being around a crowd of niggas. He was just glad that his time was almost up. He missed being out in the free world. He talked to his people all the time, but since he was five and a half hours away from Chicago, he didn't get many visits. Blake, Faith, and Deja did visit him a few times in the beginning, but it was hard seeing them only for two hours, so he asked them to stop.

Faith did make sure to mail him updated pictures of their son and letters on a regular. He heard from Ricky that she had a man now, and he was happy for her. He hoped that meant she wouldn't get in his way when he got home and they could just co-parent for the sake of his son. She didn't get the abortion like he told her to, but she did end up having a miscarriage. He hated she went through that, but at the same time, he wasn't sad about her not having the baby.

Nasir sat and drew for a couple hours, then lay down to take a nap. He was waiting for night shift to come in so that he could use one of the correctional officers' phones. He was cool with the two females that covered his block at night. He needed to talk to Reign, or he was going to go crazy over the next couple days.

Like clockwork, Officer Evans came strolling over to his cell at one o'clock a.m. That was the time she always let him out of the cell for an hour. She picked that time because it was lights out, so all of the inmates were asleep, and her partner was on her lunch break.

Nasir followed Officer Evans into their secret spot. She closed and locked the door, then crashed her lips into his. He removed her uniform, and she stood before him in a black lace lingerie set. He took the time to admire her.

Officer Evans was a dark-skinned, slim-thick chick with a pretty face and dark-brown eyes. He was drawn to her beauty when he got transferred to the prison two and a half years ago. At first, it started off as innocent flirting between them, then Nasir decided to test the waters and ask her when he could hit. At first, she was acting nervous, then one night, she came and let him out of his cell. All it took was one time of him giving her the dick, and she was letting him fuck whenever he wanted and giving him favors.

Nasir picked her up, and she wrapped her long legs around his waist. He buried his head in her breasts and she let out a slight moan. He slid his hand down and gently massaged her clit, causing her to grind on his fingers. When she was nice and moist, she climbed down and pulled his pants down. She dropped to her knees and sucked his dick until he grew in her mouth. When he was close to cumming, he pushed her out of the way and leaned her over the table before plunging his manhood inside her. It had been a week since he dipped off with her because she was on vacation, so he was trying his best not to cum before her.

Nasir reached around and rubbed her clit as he fucked her harder until she was cumming on his dick. He only lasted about five more minutes before he came behind her. The sensation of his nut was making her whimper as she came again. He stuck his hand over her mouth to muffle the sounds.

Nasir pulled his pants up, and Officer Evans handed him her

phone before slipping out so that she could go clean herself up. He waited about a minute then dialed Reign's number.

"Hello," Reign answered groggily.

"Oh, so your phone does work. You just been ignoring me," Nasir said.

"I haven't been ignoring you, Nasir. I've been busy and in meetings the times you call. I don't have a reason to hide anything from you."

"Okay, so you're not hiding that you're in a relationship now?"

"No, I'm not hiding that. I don't have to tell you all of my business. It's one thirty in the morning, and you calling me on some bullshit."

"Whatever. You better have your fun with that nigga while you can because daddy's coming home soon, and you know what time it is," Nasir told her.

"Boy, bye. You are not my daddy. I have to get up in the morning and my man looking at me crazy for being on the phone with you this late, so I'll talk to you when you come home to give you all your stuff," Reign said before hanging up the phone on him.

Nasir looked at the phone and almost threw it until he remembered that it wasn't his. He couldn't believe Reign would try to play him like that. He thought everything was good between them. She kept the money on his books, and he sent the money to Faith every month. She followed every instruction he told her except the one about not getting serious with anyone. He didn't care what she said though. He wasn't going out without a fight. He was going to do what he had to do to get his woman back.

"Hey, baby. Is everything okay?" Officer Evans asked.

"Yeah. I just had to check on something," Nasir replied. He was so lost in his thoughts that he didn't realize she was back in the room.

"Okay, good. I talked to my supervisor today, and my request to transfer to Chicago was approved. I'll start at the county jail in three months. My last day here is a week before you're released. I was thinking I'll stay here until you're released, then we can ride to Chicago together. I don't have a house out there yet, so me and our daughter could just move in with you. It will give you a chance to get to know her, and we could be a family." She smiled.

"I don't know about that. I'm looking forward to meeting her, but I'm not sure if moving in together is a good look right now. I can have my sister find a place for y'all, and it'll be ready when you get there," Nasir offered.

"Really, Nasir? It's not a good look? How the fuck do you think it looks on my part when I have to hide who my baby's father is from my family and friends because I can't tell them that I fell in love with an inmate? Do you realize I'm risking my career to be with you?" she cried.

"You're right. I'm sorry. It's just a lot of shit went down when I got locked up. I don't even know what my living situation is going to look like when I get home," Nasir half lied.

The truth was, Blake sold their grandmother's house, and Reign found a house for him a couple weeks ago already, and they put it in Deja's name. No one knew about his daughter, and there was no way he would get Reign back if she found out he had another kid.

When he first found out that he'd gotten Officer Evans pregnant, he told her to get an abortion, but she refused. He couldn't believe she was stupid enough to fuck him on the regular raw while she wasn't on birth control knowing the consequences of what would happen if anybody found out. She said she didn't care, and she wanted her baby. There was nothing he could do about it, and he needed her help while he was locked up, so he just went with the flow. He didn't see them as being in a relationship, but told him that she loved him all the time. He didn't understand how he always ended up with delusional women.

"Have you at least talked to Reign about us yet?"

"No. I told you that this isn't something that I can do over the phone. I'll talk to her when I get home," Nasir lied.

Nasir wasn't one to lie to other females about his relationship status. When he first talked to Officer Evans before they started fucking, he told her all about Reign and their relationship. He lied and told her that he couldn't get serious with her because he had a fiancée waiting for him at home. She was cool with it in the beginning, but after she had the baby, all of that changed. She demanded he break things off with Reign so they could be together. Every time she brought Reign up, he'd lie and tell her not to worry about it. He didn't know why she didn't realize she was just something to help his time go by so he didn't have to beat his meat on the regular. He wished she was like her coworker and knew how to play her part. When she wanted him to give her some D, she snuck condoms in because she wasn't about to ruin her life for him, and he was cool with that.

"Alright, baby, I don't mean to pester you. It's just the time I've been waiting for is finally here, and I don't want anything to mess it up. I can't wait until we can go out on dates and make love all over our house." She beamed before kissing him on the lips.

"I got you, baby," Nasir replied to her. He looked up at the clock, and it was ten minutes to two. He had to hurry up and get back to his cell before the other CO got off lunch. He had gone all that time without them knowing he was fucking both of them, and he wanted to leave it that way.

When Nasir made it back to his cell, he lay across his bunk and closed his eyes. He had so much shit to deal with when he got home, and he wasn't sure where to start. He could always ghost Officer Evans since she didn't have a phone number or current address on him, but then, that would make him a dead-beat dad because he'd be ghosting his daughter, and no matter how much of an asshole he was, he couldn't do that. He'd just have to figure out a way to be in his daughter's life without being with her mother.

❧ 19 ❧

Two months passed since Nasir called Reign. He had been calling her every day nonstop, and she was ready to block to him. He was acting like a crazed stalker, and she didn't know what to do. She tried having a civilized conversation with him, but it always ended in an argument, so she gave up. She could only imagine how he was going to act once he got out. It was starting to stress her out and put a strain on her relationship with Sincere.

Reign didn't know what was going on with Sincere lately. It felt like he was distancing himself from her, and she didn't like it. They talked every day, but they were only seeing each other on the weekend, if that. He didn't bring the subject back up of them moving together, and neither did she. She figured he was feeling some type of way about the way Nasir had been calling her, but he assured her it wasn't that.

Reign used the extra time she had to bury herself in her work. She had been working with her team and contractors around the clock to make sure that everything was ready for her grand opening. She needed everything to go smoothly.

"Hey, babes. Are you almost ready?" Kehlani asked, interrupting Reign's thoughts.

"Yeah. Give me about five minutes," Reign replied.

Reign grabbed her silver and black mini bodycon dress and pulled it over her head. It hugged her curves perfectly like it was made just for her. The four-inch silver YSL stilettos she put on made her ass sit higher and her toned legs pop out more. A makeup artist already came and did her makeup. She had a natural look done with silver eyeshadow around the eyes, and her long hair was in spiral curls. Normally, she didn't put so much care into her appearance, because she was always dancing, so she sweated a lot, but since it was her grand opening, Kehlani convinced her to go the extra mile. She was glad she did because she had never felt so beautiful in her life.

Reign grabbed her purse and was about to leave out her room when her phone started to ring. She looked down at it and saw it was Sincere.

"Hello," Reign answered.

"Hey, baby. I was calling to let you know that I might be a few minutes late for your grand opening, but I will be there," Sincere said.

"Really, Sin? You know how important today is for me. What is going on with you? Do you not want to be with anymore or something?" Reign asked.

"What? Why would you ask me that, Reign? You know I love you," he said.

"You can't possibly be wondering why I asked you that. We see each other less now than before we got into a relationship, and hell, you were only coming up here for one week out of the month. You've been in Memphis all week, and instead of you coming to see me yesterday after you landed, you tell me you're tired and staying at home. Instead of you coming here to take me to my grand opening, I'm riding with Kehlani, and you're going to be late. I've been in a wishy-washy relationship before. I'm older now, and I refuse to put up with that shit. I don't give a fuck how much I love you," Reign's voice cracked.

Sin sighed before responding back to Reign.

"I'm not trying to be wishy-washy. I really was tired, Reign, but you're right. That's not an excuse. It's just been stressful trying to transition from Memphis to here. The only reason I'm going to be late today is because my mother and stepfather called me to their house, and things took a little longer than I expected."

"Whatever, Sincere. I'll see you when you show up. If not, oh well," Reign replied before hanging up.

Reign couldn't hold back the tears that started to fall from her eyes anymore.

"Reign, come on. We have to go, or we're going to be late," Kehlani said.

"Okay. Here I come." Reign sniffled.

Kehlani walked over to Reign and looked in her eyes.

"What's wrong? You look too beautiful to be crying. Today is a big accomplishment for you. You're not supposed to be letting anybody ruin it," Kehlani told her.

"I know. I'm just so emotional and stressed right now. I feel like Sincere is hiding something from me, and I don't know what it is," Reign cried.

"Reign, you know all this stress isn't good for you. You two need to sit down and talk about everything, but not today. You worked too damn hard to let Sincere or anybody else fuck this up. We about to clean you up, and then you're going to fix your crown and show them who the fuck you are. You worked your ass off and made this happen without the help of any of those niggas. Remember, just because you want him don't mean you need him," Kehlani told her.

Reign smiled, then hugged her friend. Meeting Kehlani in college was one of the best things that could have happened to her. Kehlani was the one friend that she knew she could count on, no matter what. Reign could be in the wrong and she'd have her back, but once they were in private, she'd call her out on her shit. She'd never front her off in front of other people like Eve did. Whenever Reign was down, Kehlani made sure to remind her that she was a bad bitch.

Kehlani helped Reign fix her makeup, then she put in a few eyedrops to clear her eyes up, and she looked as good as new. Reign grabbed her purse, and they headed out of the house to the waiting car. Since it was Reign's big day, Mason didn't want them driving, so he booked a car service for them.

Reign's studio was only twenty minutes from where she lived. The closer she got, the more nervous she was. Before she knew it, the driver was pulling up front, and Kehlani was talking her shoulder.

"Remember, take a deep breath, hold your shoulders back, keep your head up, and smile," Kehlani coached her.

Reign climbed out of the car and did exactly what Kehlani told her to do. They entered the studio, and it was already packed with people. Servers were going around, handing out glasses of champagne and appetizers. The DJ was playing music, and people were dancing and having a good time already. Her workers were going around with sign-up sheets for people to book classes, and people were in her store buying clothes.

Reign started her own line of workout clothes, equipment, and shakes. She didn't know how it would do, but she wanted to give it a try. She figured if someone forgot their clothes, they could go in her store and buy something before practice.

There was also a small café inside of the studio where people could get smoothies, shakes, and other healthy snacks.

Reign walked around and greeted her guests, then made her way over to where her family was standing.

"Hey, Reign. This place is amazing. I'm going to have to come here so that you can teach your old mama a thing or two," joked Helen.

"Thank you, Ma, and you're not old." Reign smiled.

"Reign, your mom is right. You did a great job with this place," Helen's husband, Jeremy, added.

"Thank you for everything, Jeremy. You really looked out for me when it came to finding a contractor and everything."

"You're welcome, but I told you that you don't have to keep thanking me. We're family now, so it's my job to look out for you."

Reign stood and talked to her mom and stepfather until her father and Amelia came over to them.

"Hey. Thank you for coming." Reign greeted them both with a hug.

"You're welcome, sweetheart. You know there's nowhere else I would rather be. I am so proud of you. You had a dream, and you brought it to life."

"Yes. Like I'm so overwhelmed right now at this outcome. I wasn't even expecting this many people to show up. Most of my classes are already full for the first six weeks, and I haven't opened it to the public yet."

"Your work and résumé speak for themselves. I told you that you didn't have anything to worry about," Amelia chimed in.

Reign smiled at her stepmother. She built a good relationship with her like she did her father. At first, Reign was uncomfortable being around Amelia after she caught her mother and father in bed together, but eventually, she pushed it to the back of her mind. She wasn't sure if her parents continued their affair after that day, and she really didn't care as long as they kept it away from her. None of them acted weird around each other, and Reign kept the secret to herself like she promised.

"I have to go finish greeting people as they come in. I'll make sure to come back in a little while," Reign said.

Reign walked away and talked to a few more people until she felt somebody grab herself arm and pull them into her.

"You look beautiful," Jason whispered in her ear.

Reign stepped around Jason and turned to face him.

"Thank you. You don't look too bad yourself," she replied, scanning his body.

"I miss you, Reign," Jason confessed.

"No, Jason. We're not doing this again. We're too old to be playing this game. I'm in a relationship now, and I'm happy. My relationship with Sincere isn't like the one I had with Nasir."

"I hear you, and I can respect that, but answer me this. What are you doing at your event alone? Don't he know it's niggas like me in the shadows waiting to take his spot?" Jason smirked.

"He'll be here in a little while, and he knows that niggas are lurking, but he also knows his spot is secure," she said, smirking back.

"Okay, but you know where to find me if it doesn't work out between you two." Jason leaned over and kissed Reign on the cheek before walking away.

Reign smiled slightly, then looked up and locked eyes with a pissed-off Sincere. She was about to walk over and approach him until she saw Mason walk over to him first. They laughed, then exchanged a brotherly hug. She had no idea that they had even known each other. She needed to know what that was all about.

Reign grabbed a glass of champagne from one of the servers and sipped a little, then walked over to her brother and Sincere.

"Hey, baby sis. I'm sorry I'm late. I had to pick up your gift." Mason handed Reign the small gift bag. She opened it and pulled out a Cartier box. She opened it, and there was a yellow-gold Cartier bracelet inside.

"Oh my God. Thank you so much. You're the best big brother in the world." Reign beamed. She was so excited about her gift that she forgot to see how Mason and Sincere knew each other.

"You're welcome. I had to get you a boss ass gift since you a boss now. While you're over here, let me introduce you to my homie Sincere. We grew up together and do business with each other," Mason told her.

"Hey. It's nice to meet you," Reign spoke to Sincere, acting as if she didn't know him. She couldn't wait until she got him alone, because she had no idea Sincere dipped into illegal business because she knew Sin didn't work at any of the car washes or auto body shops that Mason owned.

Sincere looked at her confused, but then he played along as well.

"Nice to meet you too. I'm impressed with your spot. If you ever need investors, let me know." Sincere pulled a business card from his pocket and was about to hand it to Reign, but Mason intervened and took it.

"Nah. She's good. She doesn't need to be reaching out to you. You know the rules. My sisters aren't allowed to affiliate with my friends. It's bad enough she dated your cousin Nas and that nigga crazy behind her. Bedsides, you're married to Destiny, so that would be a disaster waiting to happen," Mason said.

Reign started to choke on the champagne she had in her mouth after hearing those words.

"Are you okay?" Mason asked as he tapped her on the back.

"Yeah. It just went down the wrong pipe. Give me a minute to go get myself together."

Reign hurriedly walked away and headed toward her office before anyone could stop her.

Mason's words played in her head over and over. Not only was Sincere related to Nasir, but he was married to that bitch Destiny.

Reign sat on the edge of her desk for about two minutes before there was a knock at the door.

"Yeah," Reign called out.

"Can I come in? We need to talk," Sincere said.

Reign got up and opened the door for him, then stepped to the side. As soon as the door was closed, she went in on his ass.

"Oh, now you want to talk. I was doing fine before your ass blew back into my life. How the fuck could you not tell me that you're married? You didn't even give me the chance to decide if I wanted to be your mistress," Reign yelled.

"It's not like that, Reign. I am married, but we're in the middle of a divorce."

"You should have fucking came and asked to be with me after the divorce then. This is some bullshit, Sincere. I can't even fucking introduce you as my man."

"I know, and I'm sorry. I've been trying to find the right way to tell you. That's why I've been so distant because it breaks my heart to look in your eyes every day knowing I was keeping a secret from you."

"Are you still fucking her? Is that why you didn't come see me last night?"

"What? Of course not. I would never cheat on you. I haven't slept with her in almost four months. She cheated on me, and I tried to forgive her then I found out she had an abortion. After that, I couldn't stand to be around her, so that's when I came out here straight to you. I never should have even married her. At the time, you weren't ready to be with me, and she claimed to want everything I did, but afterward, I found out it was all a lie."

"We've been together here for almost three months, so what's holding this divorce up?"

"She doesn't want to sign the papers. She keeps lying to my mama about things, which is why I had to see her and my stepfather before I got here."

Reign sank down in the chair and started to cry. She hated how emotional she was lately. It made her feel weak, and she hated it.

"I'm so sorry, Reign. I will fix this. Please don't leave me, baby. I'll make sure she signs the papers," he promised her.

Something clicked in Reign, and her emotions went from sad to anger. Kehlani's words resonated in her head. She wasn't the bitch that sat around and cried over a nigga. She got through the last few years without needing one. She was a bad bitch, and nobody could take that away from her.

Reign stood from her seat and stood in Sincere's face.

"This is so fucked up, Sincere. You better handle this shit fast because I'm six weeks pregnant." Reign dropped the bomb on Sincere, then walked out of the office.

Reign was about to continue her story, when there was a tap on her shoulder. She had been so engrossed in it she never looked at the timer on the back wall. It was time for one of the other guest speakers to come up.

"Oh, come on now. You have to at least let her tell us how Sincere reacted to the news of her being pregnant. Or what happened when Nasir got out of jail and found out," someone from the audience shouted.

Reign hated having to leave them right there when it was just getting good, but there was one more day left of the event, and so much stuff still needed to come to light.

"I'm sorry, you all. I really am, but I promise to fill you all in on everything that went down in my next session. All of your questions will be answered."

Reign knew they were all curious to know who she ended up with in the end. Was it Jason, Nasir, Sincere, or did those three hurt her so badly that she found love in someone else? Looking back on it all now, Reign couldn't believe that she lived that life. It was like it came straight from an urban-fiction novel. She knew people judged her for the decisions she made, but she didn't care. It was her life to live. At some point, she was the true definition of young and dumb, but with everything she experienced, she turned it into a lesson.

It was funny how that thing called love worked. Sometimes it made you do the unthinkable and forgive the unimaginable. You can never sit back and comment on someone else's life about what you wouldn't do until you're in that situation yourself. Everybody was built different, and what one woman accepted, the next one wouldn't, and vice versa.

There were a few grumbles from the audience, but Reign just smiled and went back to her seat and prepared to hear Kehlani speak.

To Be Continued...

Made in the USA
Coppell, TX
17 November 2021